WATCH OVER HER

OLIVIA STEPHEN

Best —

Olivia Stephen

Editing by Jenn Wood

Formatting by Jessica Ames

Cover Design by Alexandra Davis of Alexandra Designs & Alexander Beeman

Cover Model: Lawren Beeman

Cover image copyright © 2018

Imprint: Independently published

❧

To my husband
My champion, my once in a lifetime
The one who never let me give up on pursuing my dream.

To my two amazing children
I couldn't be any prouder of the wonderful young adults you've become.

Prologue

It would be helpful, considerate really, if life would let you know ahead of time when you were about to experience one of those life-altering events. One of those moments that would irrevocably change your world in the blink of an eye. Sort of give you a heads up, or a small glimpse into your day, if you will, so you could be mentally and emotionally prepared for what was about to happen.

Life isn't that kind.

Donning my best black dress, I sit here in my dad's favorite chair, attempting to drink a glass of wine, and contemplate my decision. My heart swells with a sea of tears. Do I remain here and drink away my reality, or drive myself to my parents' funeral?

The funeral.

My life-altering event.

The one I had no idea was coming.

Blindsided.

I think a breakdown would be perfectly acceptable considering the circumstances I'm faced with right now. At twenty-two, burying both of my parents after they were killed in a car accident constitutes a bit of a mental lapse, don't you think? I mean, who would really blame me?

After a few more minutes of nothingness pass, I sluggishly drag myself out of Dad's chair. I have to do this. I'll do it for them. To be the respectful young lady they taught me to be.

I reach the sink, pouring out the contents of my glass. My stomach remains empty from days without nourishment. The wine glass slips out of my shaking hands and crashes to the floor, shattering. Just like my heart.

Making my way to the front door, I catch a glimpse of my image in the mirror above the small stand near the doorway where I keep my keys. Vacant, red, and swollen eyes stare back at me. Empty. Desolate. Hopeless.

I will struggle through this day, one second, one minute, one hour at a time. And then I will come home and succumb to the emptiness that permeates not only this house but also my soul.

I am alone.

Chapter One

RAINA

Two Years Later...

It's not that I don't want to go to the pub tonight. Honestly, it's not. But here I am, pacing back and forth in my apartment, debating on whether I should hang out with friends tonight or just stay put. I know, without a doubt, he will be there.

Zane. God, that man.

Zane is the gorgeous, brooding man who tends bar at the pub that we hit at the end of the really stressful weeks. He started working at Sam's Pub around the same time I moved to town, about eight months ago, and he's definitely intriguing. His smile never quite connects to his mysterious eyes; it's one that speaks of a hard life. Distant and disconnected. But still, it's a beautiful smile, and there's a part of me that would love to know his story.

He rocks a hard, strong body and hair that falls just so. Styled, but then again not. His perfectly chiseled jaw accentuates his face, and it's so easy for me to get lost in those serious, beautifully-colored, Caribbean blue eyes. His skin isn't covered in tattoos, but I have noticed a few when he wears a short-sleeved tee. It looks like one may be a name and a date, which makes me curious.

And when this man walks into the bar, his presence commands the room, and every girl in the place melts just a little. Especially me.

I've tried, on several occasions, to engage in some kind of conversation with him, yet he always remains distant and quiet. A simple "'Here you go, darlin'", as he hands me my drink, is about the only form of verbal communication between the two of us. Interestingly, I often catch him staring at me when he isn't busy pouring the newest tap beer or mixing some alcohol-laden drink for one of the local residents who frequent Sam's Pub. Maybe it's just a hook-up or a one-night stand kind of look, which so isn't me. Or perhaps it's something else entirely. Either way, frustrating is what it is.

So even as I continue to get ready to meet my few friends from school, swiping my lips with light pink gloss and brushing a light coat of blush on my cheeks, I make every excuse I can think of to stay home, but come up empty.

I drive off to the pub, resigned not to let him get to me tonight. I'll have Sarah, my best friend, hit the bar for our drinks while I stay rooted in my seat. I will not swing *my* eyes towards the handsome bartender in the hopes of catching *his* stunning blue ones looking my way. I'll have a drink or two then head home to my small, cozy apartment. It's the one I fell in love with when I moved to this town after the death of my parents two years ago, which left me to pick up the pieces of my life totally alone.

Sarah and I arrive at the same time, and we walk in through the heavy door, out of the cool night air. A different bartender stands behind the large wooden bar tonight, and I breathe a sigh of relief, though I can't help but also feel somewhat disappointed. My brooding, serious, bartender is nowhere to be found.

Shrugging off the disappointment, I head to the group of tables where the gang is fully immersed in a round of drinks. It's common to have live music at the pub on Friday or Saturday evenings, and the sweet sound of acoustic music can be heard coming from the amplifiers by the small elevated stage. The two men on stage, plucking their guitars and singing into the microphones, are frequent guests here, and we all enjoy their music. They are really good, and I've always felt they're wasting their time here at the pub. They have the talent, and the looks, to take their show on the road and make it big.

But alas, here they are, crooning their cover songs, sounding melodic and perfectly in tune. Actually, for a night out, to have a few drinks and talk with friends, it *is* perfect.

Chapter Two

ZANE

My patience is just about at my limit as I go about getting ready to head to the pub. I don't get many nights off from the bar, so really, I'd just rather stay home. I'm getting very little sleep and I've been thinking a great deal about my brother. It's making me tenser than I usually am.

So right now, I'm going through the motions, grabbing and putting on clean jeans and whatever unwrinkled shirt I can find. I snag a bottled water and my keys as I head out to the bar.

Friday nights are a big night for the weekday nine-to-fivers, and since Raina is a teacher, I know for certain that she and her friends will be there. Some nights, she comes in with her friend, Sarah, and I often watch her as she rolls her neck, breathing deeply, in hopes of releasing some kind of tension. She obviously takes her teaching very seriously and wants to do her best for her students. It makes me wish I could do something to make her life easier, less tense, but all I would do is just create more problems.

As I unlock my car, I stop myself for a moment. I've been

catching myself thinking about her far too often and I really need to stop. Nothing can happen with her even though I wish it could. Raina's truly an amazing woman, which makes it difficult to keep my distance. She has such a beautiful soul, I can tell, which is second only to her amazing smile. She's obviously a wonderful friend to Sarah, and I'm certain she loves the students she teaches. Even though her smile doesn't always reach her eyes, she has an air about her that radiates when she walks into a room.

And she's most definitely easy on the eye as well. Her contagious laugh, not to mention that gorgeous body, with curves in all the right places, and long, deep brown hair that frames her smiling face, makes her the sexiest woman I know. And sexy in such an unintentional way; she doesn't even have to try. Her genuine smile and the unassuming way she walks into a room makes me hard just watching her. If there has ever been a perfect woman created, it's Raina. Stunning on the outside, but most importantly, a beautiful heart.

As hard as it is to be around her sometimes, I know moving here from Raleigh was the right thing to do. But letting Raina into my life would be a disaster of the most epic kind. I could never have a relationship with her. Never.

My thoughts linger on her and the fact that I'm only supposed to simply watch her from a distance. I promised my brother that's what I would do. And *that* right there has become the biggest test of my patience.

The short drive to the bar doesn't give me a whole lot of time to do much thinking. Which, in reality, is a good thing. I figure I'll just hang at the bar with Sam, the owner, for a couple hours, keep an eye on Raina, then head back home.

I pull into my assigned parking space in the parking lot of the pub. Getting out of the car, I see Tira running up to me. I stop and close my eyes, shaking my head.

Why is she here on my night off? I can't catch a break.

And she can't seem to catch the hint. I'm not interested. She's nice looking for sure, but she irritates the shit out of me with her whining and her attitude. She's about as mean as they come when she's around other women at the bar. It's like she's competing with them for my attention.

Now, it seems, this night can't be over fast enough.

Chapter Three

RAINA

I don't even see him come in the door of the bar. I feel it. I feel that intense gaze and the heat. The dynamics of this place actually change when he's here. My eyes stay glued to my drink as the warmth in my face grows, causing my cheeks to turn even pinker than the blush I'd applied an hour earlier.

Sarah figures it out instantly and chuckles to herself. She's very well aware of the brooding bartender and the way his ocean blue eyes zero in on me when he thinks I'm not looking. She often encourages me to just let loose and "Tap that," as she puts it.

My eyes are drawn to that man like a moth to a flame. It's as though I have no choice but to look, so, without even consciously thinking about it, I steal a quick glance, and I am once again captivated by the strong man looking directly at me. His eyes connect to mine, speak to mine, somehow making me believe that he can see into my very soul. Worn and frayed jeans that hang low on his hips, and a dark blue Henley that clings to his muscles adorn a well over six-foot-tall body. He is magnificently handsome tonight.

I see his stern face, and draw in a quick breath, hoping I can recover before he notices. There is interest in his eyes, but just as I catch that, he looks away. I think about the phrase, *our eyes meet across a crowded room*, and consider how amusingly appropriate it is for this moment.

It's then, shortly after that clichéd thought, I notice he isn't alone. And my heart sinks.

Standing next to Zane, in all her glory, is Tira, who waitresses here at Sam's Pub. She is beautiful, that exotic, model type of beauty. Worldly and eccentric. I wonder why she's working in a pub in small-town North Carolina instead of strutting on some runway in Milan or Paris. That's how beautiful she is.

However, her beauty is outward only. She is a bitch, at best, and can probably give Satan himself a run for his money. I hate that she notices me looking at Zane. A smirk falls across those ruby red lips of hers and makes me feel like crawling inward and never coming out again. She quickly grabs on to Zane's arm, resting her head near his shoulder. I knew I shouldn't have come here tonight.

Sarah rolls her eyes. "Don't let that bother you. I'm here often enough and I know they're just friends."

"That glare of hers tells me something completely different," I reply.

"In her dreams. She sleeps around with every bartender here. Probably every bartender in every bar in this town and the next one over, and yet, I've never seen him leave with her. You need to put on the big girl panties and ask him out." She says it so nonchalantly it's almost laughable.

Ask him out. I briefly let that thought swim around in my head. Ask *him* out? As if. How in the world does a 24-year-old virgin go after a man...no, a Greek god, who has a Greek goddess hanging on his arm? Especially when I look like this? Not that I'm horrid looking. I'm average at best. I eat fairly well, and hit the gym or go for a long power walk when the urge hits me. I have long brunette hair, dark brown eyes, and through the magic of online tutorials and videos, I'm getting a great deal more comfortable with applying the little bit of make-up I do use. But, five-foot-five and 125 pounds is nothing compared to five-foot-nine and 110.

"Stop. I know what you're doing."

Yes, she does. Sarah knows how insecure I can be, but she also knows how much my confidence is growing. A few years ago, my ex up and left me without ever looking back. I became so self-conscious, wondering what it was about me that would cause him to fall into the arms of an older woman and take off with her. Sarah still gets pissed when I bring it up. I've never had an over-abundance of self-confidence any time in my life, and all the crap with my ex-boyfriend really took its toll.

"I know, and I'm fine," I whisper. "It isn't like he and I have ever dated. Or even had a conversation that extended beyond a few words. But it's like there's this pull toward him. I don't get it, Sarah. He's the last guy I should ever get involved with, and the fact that he can't even speak more than five words to me should be a big, red, waving flag. I don't know what the hell I'm doing even imagining being with him."

At that moment, Tira begins dragging him over to our table to say hello to the group with her sickeningly sweet voice and fake smile. I know what she's doing, staking her claim. Her hands never leave his arm. I do smile, though, when I see him pull away from her at the last minute before reaching us. Before anyone can say a word, I excuse myself to the restroom.

"I'll be right back," I say, and quickly make my exit, Sarah right on my heels.

There are some things I don't want to witness, and Zane with Tira is one of them.

I swing the bathroom door open and take a deep breath as I stand near the sink.

"What the hell, Raina?"

"I need a minute. Give me a minute to get it together."

"One minute. Then we're going back out there," she says, waving her finger, nearly poking me in the chest. "The tension between you two is so thick, and it's about time one of you did something about it. If I had to make a guess, I think that someone needs to be you."

Tell me how you really feel, Sarah. Don't hold back on my account.

She's right, though. I know for sure he won't initiate anything between us, because it's been months and he hasn't made any kind of move. But, could I do this? Could I put myself out there? Try again? All my life, people I've loved have left me, in one way or another. My grandparents are gone, my parents died in a horrific accident. Then, of course, there's the ex. Always imagining my happily ever after with him was one humongous mistake. There are no happily-ever-afters anyway.

Zane certainly doesn't scream "available" to me. Maybe he's just really shy, but I chuckle to myself. Shy is not a word *anyone* would use to describe Zane. *Serious, moody, stoic, unsettled, hot,* I rattle off quickly in my head. Those words fit. Shy? Not so much.

Sarah leaves the bathroom first. I follow behind her, stopping short when a very distraught Zane looms in front of me. His piercing stare feels as if he could devour me in a heartbeat, and I'm not sure what to think or how to feel in that moment. Of course, I decide maybe right now is the time to put myself out there.

For just an instant, those eyes soften as I look up at him,

and he visibly relaxes. But as quickly as it happens, it's over. The walls he obviously has in place are put back up, and if I had to guess, those walls are almost impenetrable.

"Hey, Raina." The way my name rolls off his tongue is sexy as sin with his rough voice. Looking up at him is intense as he stands there, one foot crossed over the other, arms folded and a broad shoulder leaning against the wall.

"Zane. Good to see you. I wondered if you'd be here tonight."

He smirks, laughing quietly to himself. "You were thinking about me?"

If you only knew.

"Well, coming here most Fridays and you bartending, I was just, you know, thinking maybe you'd be working. Looks like you're working on Tira, though." Instantly, my face reddens at the comment I let slip.

Jeez Raina, open mouth, insert foot. What the hell?

"Tira and I aren't together. Not now and not ever. We're friends, and that's all," he replies, in a tone that implies I should not question him. He pushes off the wall, causing him to stand at his full, intimidating height.

"Maybe someone should tell her that, then." I glance down and straighten my back in the hopes of looking taller and more confident, but my hands fumble with the hem of my shirt. Closing my eyes, I attempt to gather some courage. "Look, I know we see each other a lot here at the pub. We've never talked, not really. Maybe sometime we could...um, get a coffee together or something?"

Coffee? Really? Does he look like the coffee type?

I can see his back stiffen, and the look in his eyes tells me I might be way off. "Raina, you don't want coffee with me. You don't want anything with me. Trust me."

It's not surprising to hear him say that, but it does make me sad. It's like he doesn't feel he's worthy of me in some way. He doesn't really know anything about me, so it's odd he would think that.

"Maybe you shouldn't assume to know what it is I want. It's just coffee, Zane. Not a marriage proposal."

His look becomes more focused and his hand flattens quickly on the wall beside my face, leaning forward, virtually blocking me in. His lips are so close to mine, stealing the air directly from my lungs. I can barely breathe.

There is something there. Something he is ready to say. There's a storm raging in those eyes, some truth he is fighting to reveal. Fluttering isn't the word I would use to describe what my heart is doing, because it is so much more intense than that. Racing, perhaps. He closes his eyes and butterflies swirl in my stomach as I ready myself for a kiss. He is that close.

Silence fills the air.

But then the moment passes. His hand comes down along with his head. He stares at the floor and gruffly lets out a moan. He storms away with his hands in fists, and I stand there, alone again, knees shaking, unable to breathe. I get it now. I'm not enough for him.

My heart feels hollow. Something I've felt quite a bit in the past two years.

Chapter Four

RAINA

Inervously walk back to the table to finish my drink with every intention of leaving once it's empty. I sigh, left even more confused by the heightened interaction with Zane, albeit brief. His heart may have said one thing; his mind said something else entirely.

"Holy shit! God, he's intense. What *was* that?"

"Who knows," I say, as I plop back down in my seat beside Sarah, trying to shake off the rejection. "I asked him to go for coffee." I turn my body quickly to face her and roll my eyes. "Does he look like the coffee type to you? The shit that comes out of my mouth sometimes amazes me! No wonder he walked away."

"That wasn't just walking. The intensity on his face...he was ready consume you. That man has it bad for you and for whatever reason, he won't admit it."

Unfortunately, she has it all wrong. So do I. I was shot down tonight, and since I don't care for a repeat performance of that humiliation any time soon, I'll just keep my distance from now on.

"Yeah, well, it is what it is. Let's finish these and head out. I'm exhausted, and it's been a long week."

Sarah and I finish our drinks in relative silence, listening to the conversations from others at our table. The live music has stopped briefly, and as I get up to leave, one-half of the acoustic duo stops me with a hand on my arm. He glances at Sarah, smiles, then his eyes land on me.

"Hey. We just finished our second set. I was wondering if you'd like to sit with me for a drink?"

I nervously look around to find Sarah, and there she stands, an amused look on her face.

"Of course she'd like another drink. But sadly, I have to head on home to…let out the dog. Yeah, the dog."

Sarah, you don't have a dog!

"Great," says Guitar Man, looking questioningly at me. "What would you like?"

"Um…I, uh…just a glass of wine. Please. Moscato."

"Coming right up. I have a table right over there, I'll meet you after I get our drinks."

My thoughts are somewhat confused right now. Didn't Sarah *just* tell me to pull up my big girl panties and perhaps try a date with Zane? And now she's pushing for me to have drinks with Guitar Guy. She has to be the most confusing friend I've ever had. But with more experience with men than me, maybe she's onto something. I most certainly don't have a clue.

The table is off to the side of the pub, near the stage but away from most everyone else. Guitar Guy comes to sit down and introduces himself as Liam. I remembered the singers' names were Liam and Cole; I just didn't remember which was which. My attention, as of late, has obviously been on the bar.

I learn that Liam is originally from the Durham area and grew up in a musical household, both parents also being musicians. He is tall and very well-built, with shaggy blond hair and piercing eyes.

What is it with men and their eyes?

Liam is a good-looking guy, and the fact that he plays the guitar and sings make him that much more attractive. We talk, drink, and enjoy each other's company and conversation. It's easy with him, I have to admit.

And I won't, at any point in my time with Liam, address the angry look on Zane's face as he watches Liam and I interact. He is unquestionably pissed, but there's Tira sitting right next to him, ready to crawl all over him like a monkey in a tree. He's basically ignoring her, and the look on her face is one of a scorned lover. But, whatever.

Moments later, Zane rushes out the door and leaves Tira alone at the bar, nearly making a scene and clearly irritated.

"What's with Zane?" asks Liam, motioning his head toward the entrance.

"You know him?"

"Just from playing here once in a while, sure. He's been staring at you all night. Are you two dating?"

I try my best not to stare at the door where Zane just stormed out. "Oh God, no. Not dating. At all. He barely even talks to me. Really. I have no idea what's up," I say nervously, trying to turn this conversation around. "So, y'all sounded great tonight. Loved your music. It's been a long week, so anything would sound good...I mean, you weren't bad..."

You can shut up anytime now. Could this night get any worse?

Liam chuckles, tilting his head to the side. "Thank you, I think."

I take a deep breath and scoot my chair back. "I think it's about time I head out. Thank you for the drinks. It was great to meet you. I'll probably see you again next time you play here."

"Sounds great. How about this Friday? We're scheduled to play at eight and I'd love to see you again."

"Um, okay. Perfect. I'll see you then."

My steps are quick as I make my way to the car, replaying this crazy night over and over in my mind. And I know there will be very little sleep tonight.

Chapter Five

ZANE

My bed provides no comfort to me again tonight. Sleep eludes me. No wonder I'm constantly irritated. Sleepless nights do not help my mood at all, but there are so many things that have happened in my life that keep my mind agitated and troubled, which certainly doesn't allow for a good night's rest.

I can't help but think of Raina. I hurt her tonight. I saw those eyes, as embarrassment passed over them, as she closed them when I stepped away, right before I allowed my mouth to devour hers. Jesus, I went from irritable to asshole in a matter of seconds. But I had no choice.

My thoughts circle back to her over and over again. For a moment, I imagine her talking to me and enjoying my company, the way she enjoyed Liam's. What I wouldn't give to be the one she smiled at.

I allow my mind to wander, and I imagine taking her to a romantic dinner, holding her hand, and bringing her back to my apartment. I anticipate the wild look in her eyes as I begin to kiss her slowly, but eagerly, my tongue caressing the softness right behind her ear. I can almost hear the hitch in her breath as she responds to my fingers coming in contact with her satiny skin. My roughened hands would strip her body of clothing, then trace every line and curve of her beautiful physique, possibly twice. She would straddle my lap, rubbing herself against me. Tangling her hands in my hair, her touch would set me on fire, I know, and digging her nails into my back, she would arch hers and cry out, finding her release, as I relentlessly grind against her core. Eventually, I would lead her back to the bedroom, and there we would lose ourselves in each other. Her body would shake, and she would gasp while I drive into her over, and over again, giving her pleasure like she's never known.

It would be spectacular, life-altering.

Shit. I have to stop thinking like this.

My Raina is not the kind of girl you have a one night stand with. She is the girl you make mad, passionate love to night after night. She's also the girl who deserves the fairy tale...not the nightmare that is my life.

Reality sets in again as I open my eyes from the sensual scene that just played itself out in my head. She's way too good for someone with a black soul like mine. Too many skeletons in this closet rattling around like a wind chime in a hurricane for me to be comfortable in any kind of relationship with her. If she knew half the shit that went on in my life, she'd run far, far away. Liam is so much better for her than me, and fuck all, if that doesn't make me want her even more.

I've been watching her for so long now that it's getting harder and harder to stay away from her, and even more difficult to ignore my feelings. But I promised my brother I'd keep my distance from her. I owe it to him. Hell, even from the grave he still haunts me.

A cold drink sounds good right about now, as does a quiet moment on the balcony of my apartment. I check my phone again for a message from Tira, to be sure she made it home. I know she was pissed when I left, and I know she saw me glaring at Liam. But she also knows where we stand. Friends, and *not* with benefits. She's been coming on to me for weeks now, and I can spot a clinger a mile away.

She doesn't hold a candle to Raina anyway. My feelings for Tira could never come close to what I could feel with Raina, and that's the problem. I can't have feelings for Raina. Too many complications and too many obstacles to overcome to even consider getting close to her. Even knowing that, I still can't help but feel a pull, on some subconscious level, toward her. Like her soul belongs to me.

A chill penetrates my bones as I stand outside, overtaking the heat from the story that just played out with Raina in my mind. The chill is not just because of the temperatures, though. For some reason, memories of the night I found Zander are surfacing, and I know I won't be able to get them out of my head. It's like a bad movie playing over and over. Some days, it feels like I'll never be able to escape this nightmare. I never want to forget my brother, but I wish I could just move on with my life. Why do things always have to be so fucked up for me? It's a never-ending roller coaster of emotions that I can't get off.

My phone chimes with a new message from Tira.

TIRA: Home. Thanks for leaving me, Zane! WTF??

Great. One less thing to worry about. She's home safe.

ZANE: K.

My response is brief. And that's all she'll get from me.

Chapter Six

RAINA

The week flies by, which is a rarity as a teacher. Some weeks seem like they'll never end, especially when the littles are having a difficult week. Storms, full moons, spirit weeks, birthdays; you name it, and it throws their minds into an alternate universe. After-school meetings and conferences are keeping me quite busy. I'm looking forward to tonight's get-together with Liam, and I don't even entertain the chances of running into Zane. Much. After our last little rendezvous outside the bathroom, I figure it's time to move on. Nothing here to see, folks.

Liam's first set starts at 8:00, and the pub is busy. I push through a small crowd as I make my way toward him. He already has my drink at the table waiting for me and for that, I am grateful because the less time I spend at the bar near Zane, the better. Liam shoots me a beautiful smile and nods his head acknowledging my presence. He and his buddy sound amazing again tonight, and play some of my favorite songs. He looks at me often as he plays and smiles just a bit, which makes me a tad giddy, as though I'm some sort of quirky teenager again.

However, to be honest, it doesn't give me that butterflies-have-taken-up-residence-in-my-stomach feeling I get when I'm near Zane.

We talk in between sets, and I have to admit that I do enjoy his company. Liam would make a great friend. But that's about it as far this relationship will ever develop.

Glancing over at the bar, again, I notice Zane and that familiar, irritated stare. The one that says he'd like to take me home and do some fairly indecent things to me, but he's too confused or too reluctant to allow himself to do it. The back and forth with him is tiring. So, I do my best to keep my eyes on the stage and off the solemn man behind the bar.

The night goes on like this, our eyes glancing back and forth, and I'm having a hard time being in the same room with him right now. I decide that once Liam finishes his set, I'll make an excuse to say goodbye and leave. I'm certain he's not ready for me to head home quite so early, but I really do need to get out of here.

He walks back toward our table after a few more songs and takes a seat right next to mine.

"Liam, thank you so much for a great evening. I had a good time, but I need to get home." I'm trying to smile, but it just doesn't reach my eyes and I know it.

"I can't say I'm ready for our night to be ending now. But I think I understand." He looks toward the bar and then takes my hand in his, rubbing his thumb on mine. "You're a beautiful girl, Raina. You deserve to be happy."

I feel like such a shit for doing this to him. He's a great guy, good-looking too, and deserves so much more.

I stand, giving him a quick kiss on the cheek. "I'll text you and let you know I made it home, okay," I say quickly, then head out the door. Once outside, I take a deep breath, breathing in the cool evening air. Closing my eyes for a moment, I focus on the stillness of the night. I try to center myself and quiet my mind.

As I reach my car, someone calls out my name. Turning around, I see Zane heading toward me. He moves hastily and reaches me within seconds.

"You're leaving. Why didn't you come up to the bar to get your own drinks?" he asks with a scowl on his face.

"Liam bought my drinks. I figured your decision to push me away last weekend was enough. I don't need to be told again. I thought that's what you wanted...for me to keep away from you."

Zane stands in front of me, all man, with his eyes turned upward as though looking into the heavens. When he lowers his head, I witness a tormented look marring his face. And even with that look, I think I could fall into those eyes, never to return. This man wants me, I know; I see it clearly. But whatever it is that's holding him back has him in tied in knots. I see the struggle in his stance and in the way he sways back and forth from foot to foot. He is in constant turmoil with himself, and I'd love to know why. However, it's not my business. So, for the moment, I let it go.

"What do you want?" I ask, quietly, hesitantly.

"You. I want you, Raina," he says in a voice that's barely a whisper. So soft, I almost don't hear it, even as close to me as he is.

"That's hard for me to believe, considering how last weekend's short conversation went between the two of us." Honestly, I don't know how to process what he said. It's intriguing he's admitted that thought out loud. "We've been dancing around each other for months now. I offered a coffee date, and you turned me down. I'm not quite sure what you want, and frankly it's confusing as hell." I take a step back to distance myself from this confusing encounter.

Zane's having none of that. He steps toward me, eliminating the space between us. "Look. It's not that simple. There are things you don't know."

I shake my head and consider the things he doesn't know about me. My eyes find his and I pause to calm my voice. "We all have issues, Zane. Generally, when one has an issue or a problem, one works through it on one's own, or with someone else, to resolve it. There are things you don't know about me either. My life is far from perfect."

His remorseful eyes penetrate mine, then he quickly glances away, almost as if he knows. But no one here knows, except Sarah. I've done a good job keeping that locked down. My parents' death is my own to deal with. Some days, it's fairly easy to manage, and others, it's all I can do to get through the day. The fewer people who know about it, the less time I have to spend explaining it all again. Living through it once was enough.

"I have to go," I say. "Is there anything else?"

"Yes. Coffee."

What?

"Meet me for coffee tomorrow, at the new coffee shop downtown. Around ten," he demands, moving closer.

"Are you sure that's what you want?"

"No. Not at all," he whispers as he looks back again to the sky. "But I promise I'll be there waiting for you."

And with that, he turns to head back into the pub, shaking his head, clearly debating on whether he should have even come outside to see me. I'm left with my feet stock-still, wondering what just happened. I wrap my jacket around my shoulders and slowly make my way to the car, considering Zane's words. He says he's not sure he wants to meet me, but promises he'll be there.

And men say women are confusing. We've got nothing on this man.

Chapter Seven

ZANE

What in the hell am I thinking? The more I find myself near this woman, the more my resolve crumbles. I'm supposed to keep an eye on her. Make sure she's okay and that she's moving on. Getting involved more than that is not part of the plan. But now, I'm risking blowing that all to shit.

Personally, I think coffee sucks. But if that piss tasting drink gets me some time with Raina, then I'll gladly suck down a gallon. My head's like a fucking treadmill right now. Running, running, running, and going nowhere. Do I spend time with her, or don't I? Jesus, I can't figure this shit out.

Back in the bar, I turn to Sam, the other bartender for the night, and also the owner of the pub, and the look on his face tells me he's got questions. He smirks and shakes his head at me, but I'm in no mood tonight to get into anything remotely close to my issues with Raina.

"The fuck, man? You finally hookin' up with her? 'Bout time!" I don't miss the grin on his face as he pours another draft for a customer.

Staying busy is important right now, so washing empty

beer mugs tops my list of things to do. "Not gettin' into it man. Let it go." My aggravated reply causes him to laugh out loud.

"Okay, dude. Whatever. Just be careful with her. She's a real sweetheart and most definitely doesn't need shit from the grumpy ass that is you," he says, pointing in my direction. "Be nice to her. And for God's sake, don't lead her on. I know how closed off you are. I ain't asked a thing about your past, but by the looks of it, you got some troubles. I'll leave it at that."

"Thanks for the unsolicited advice. I'm not a dick, man. Everything will be fine."

And in what world will this situation ever be fine?

The night drags on and my thoughts constantly return to Raina. She looked beautiful again tonight meeting up with that douche, Liam. He's not a douche, really; he's a good guy. The kind of guy who Raina should fall in love with. He's got his shit together, which is the complete opposite of me.

It isn't any wonder Liam is drawn to her. Raina has no idea what she does to the opposite sex, or the same sex, for that matter. She turns the heads of every guy, and some girls, in the pub when she shows up. She's not only physically beautiful but on the inside, she is as genuine and compassionate as they come. She's like a bright light in a darkened world. Someone who sees the good through all the bad that has invaded her life. This light, this angel, has taken up residence in my mind and damn, I can't get her out. Not that I want to.

However, I've made promises that I feel like I'm going back on, which is creating somewhat of a dilemma. And that thought causes me to shake my head and laugh. Figuring out whether to have whiskey or beer is a dilemma. This is not a dilemma; it's a shitstorm. And I'm right smack in the fuckin' middle of it. I've put myself there, and now I have to deal.

Sam and I close up the bar around two in the morning and I head home. Once inside my apartment, I hit the fridge for a bottled water, then pull out the letter from my brother and read his last words to me again, and again, and again. It should be a reminder to me that I can't fall in love with Raina no matter what. He wanted my forgiveness, and for me to watch over the girl he took everything from. He was so distraught and overcome with guilt, that overdosing on pills and vodka was the only choice he thought he had. That night keeps playing over and over in my head, like a fucking broken record. Those memories haunt me. Coming to terms with his suicide may never happen for me. Fuck, I miss him.

So, I'll stick to my promise to just keep an eye on Raina. At least, I'll try like hell. It was never a question that I would make sure she was okay. In the wake of my brother's mistakes, I feel like I owe Raina that much. I don't owe her another broken heart in the process, which is what she'll get if she falls in love with me. If…when…she finds out the secret I've been keeping, she'll never be able to forgive me. Any relationship we forge together will shatter.

Contemplating my decision to ask Raina to meet me at the coffee shop has my head in a jumbled mess. What the hell do I do now?

I WAKE to find myself still on the sofa, in the same clothes from last night. The morning sun shines brightly through the curtains on the windows of my small apartment. The apartment that's one block down from Raina's, which I chose on purpose, in order to be closer to her. It's December, and although the sun is out, temperatures are beginning to get colder by the week. I get up to hit the shower, knowing in a few hours, I'll be meeting Raina for coffee. My mind is still a fucking mess, and I can't make sense of any of it. I've watched over this angel from a distance for almost two years now, and I'm getting tired of fighting my feelings for her. Yet, even as I speak this truth, I know there is only one way this can end. And it's bad.

Chapter Eight

RAINA

It's nearing ten o'clock, and I'm at the coffee shop, eagerly waiting for Zane. It's a quaint little place, with bistro-style tables, and flavors and types of coffees galore. I sit near the window to see out to the main street, thinking I'd have a good view of the locals making their way around the town on this sunny December morning. Something to keep my mind occupied.

What I eventually have, is a view of Zane as he pulls into a parking space. He stays seated in his car, head down, breathing deeply, obviously debating with himself as to whether or not he should meet me. Those feelings of inadequacy began to claw at me again. Feelings I haven't had since I had finally moved on from ex and his cheating ass.

But what I observe in the next moment is quite a surprise. Zane emerges from his car and when his eyes meet mine through the coffee shop window, he smiles the most brilliant smile I think I have ever seen. Those white teeth sparkle in the sunlight. In his eyes, there is a look of adoration, and perhaps even hope. Far, far different from what I'd seen in the past.

He walks through the door and moves toward my table, like a man on a mission, and takes a seat. For the first time since I met Zane, he looks comfortable. Quite the change from the times I'd been around him before. It makes me feel like there is a possibility that something between us may work out. At the very least, we could be friends. More would be better, but baby steps.

"Hey. You made it," I say as he pulls out his chair to have a seat. The tables here are small, and his knees touch mine as he sits. I like it that he doesn't move them. I've never believed in that spark that happens when two people touch, but I'll be damned if it didn't just happen. My eyes meet his, and I know. I know he felt the same thing.

"Yep. Told you I'd be here," he replies, clearing his throat.

Jesus, even that's sexy.

The waitress saunters up to our table with the same look most women get when they see Zane. "What can I get you?" She's just as affected as the rest of the female population when he shoots his smile her way.

Zane looks again and notices I already have my coffee. "One coffee. Two banana muffins."

"Got it, sugar." She giggles, and now I'm immediately curious as to why some women feel as though it's okay to flirt with a man who is already sitting with a woman. Zane doesn't miss my irritated look and laughs under his breath. He takes a second to look directly at me, a serious look so that I know how he feels about the overzealous waitress. And then it changes into something else entirely, as if he's seeing me for the first time. It's a little disconcerting and I'm not sure why.

"So, you a coffee fan?" I ask, wanting to move on from the seriousness of the moment.

"Not in the least. But I'll give it another go. Just glad to be here with you, so I figure since I'm in a coffee shop, you know...when in Rome."

"They have other drinks, silly. I'm a teacher, so coffee is a staple. Part of the job."

Zane's sincere laugh makes me smile.

"You have a beautiful smile, Raina. You should smile all the time. You deserve someone who can make you smile like that every day." He moves around restlessly in his chair, probably rethinking that comment he just made.

"And that's not you?"

"That will never be me." He looks straight into my eyes like he's trying to gauge my reply.

The moment is interrupted by the flirtatious waitress and her annoying giggle. "Here ya go, sugar. Anything else?"

Zane closes his eyes and shakes his head, then tilts his head, staring directly at her, not blinking. He's clearly annoyed by her demeanor and his look dismisses her. I don't miss the way her eyes shift around uncomfortably. With a timid smile, she turns abruptly and walks towards another table to check on other customers.

Trying to lighten the mood, I clear my throat and I start a conversation that will hopefully help me get to know more about this man. "I'm glad you asked me to meet you. I'd really like to get to know you better."

I see the struggle on his face, and he leans back and runs his hand through his hair. Which is also sexy.

Is there anything non-sexy about this man?

Zane takes a deep breath and lets it out before reaching for his coffee, his knee bouncing nervously up and down. He takes a sip, winces, and I smile knowing he really just isn't into the coffee scene at all, but it's cute how he does this for me.

"Not much to tell. My dad doesn't live around here. Neither does, um...my brother. Mom took off a long time ago. Couldn't deal with dad's shit, I guess. Made her life miserable. I grew up, moved here, and started tending bar. That's about it."

"So, the Cliffs Notes version of Zane's life. Do you live alone?"

"Yep," he says. "Same as you."

I hesitate just for a moment, wondering about what he just said.

"How do you know I live alone"

"Just, you know, you always meet your friend when you come to the pub, so I figured you didn't live with her. Just a guess. What about you? What makes Raina such an interesting person?"

I laugh. Interesting? Funny choice of words.

"I enjoy teaching. I've always had a passion for working with kids. It's stressful, but I believe when you have a calling to teach, it's just what you do. Sarah is my best friend. We went to college together. And you're right that I live alone. I moved here from Raleigh for a teaching job after...after some things happened." Tears begin to take hold. I take a deep breath and look down at my empty coffee cup.

Please, not here! Not now!

"I'm just gonna run up to the counter for a quick refill." I hurriedly make my way to the counter for another cup where I take a few deep breaths, getting my emotions in check. After getting my refill, I head back to the table, feeling somewhat under control. I manage to keep the tears at bay and for that, I'm grateful.

Zane stands as I make my way back to the table. His hand touches mine, moving his thumb up and down along my wrist. Immediately, I feel comforted. "Are you okay? I didn't mean to upset you."

"All good. Just some memories that catch up with me

every now and then." I take a few sips of my coffee and try not to think of the shit in my past.

"You can tell me, you know. I may look like a bad-ass," he says, smiling and wiggling his eyebrows, "but I've got two good ears for listening."

I laugh out loud at that comment. "A bad-ass, huh? Well, Mr. Bad-ass, how about we take a stroll on the Riverwalk," I say, taking another sip of coffee. "This cup isn't nearly as good as the first, and I'm ready to head out before our waitress comes back and joins you on your side of the table for her break."

Zane smiles again. "Ah, yes, the waitress. Well then, let's get out of here so I don't have to let her down by telling her I'm spending my day with the prettiest girl in Hillsborough."

I chuckle to myself and feel a bit flushed at his compliment. It's good, though, to see him more relaxed and happy. I don't know what has happened in his life, besides the fact that he had a real twat for a dad, but whatever the circumstances are that he constantly thinks about, they've done a number on him. He said I deserve to smile every day. Well, the same goes for him.

We put on our coats, exit the coffee shop, and walk silently across the street, heading to the two-mile walkway along the Eno River. My heart beats wildly as he reaches out for me, linking our hands together. We begin to make our way along the bank of the river, hand in hand, with the quietness of the flowing water beside us and a cold breeze blowing the brown strands of hair from my face. A few walkers and joggers pass us by as they make their way along the trail, as do a few couples holding hands and enjoying each other's company. I think that's how Zane and I must look to them. We are enjoying each other's company, true, but I get the feeling the two of us aren't quite like those couples.

The chill in the air feels like the onset of winter, and even though we're in the south, North Carolina doesn't mean balmy temperatures year-round. We get our share of colder weather. I wrap my sweater around me a little tighter to fight off the cool breeze, then quickly reach for Zane's hand again. I feel comfortable like that.

As we move on along the Riverwalk, I'm leery of interrupting the silence, our quiet time together, as I'm not sure exactly what he is thinking.

"Do you like being outside and taking walks?" he asks suddenly.

"Sure. I mean, even though this time of year is cooler, it still feels good. Walking here is a good way to clear my head when it gets full of junk. How about you?"

Zane slows our pace and glances my way. "I like to run. Like you said, it's a good way to clear away crap I hate thinking about."

We continue on, Zane holding my hand. Even as mysterious as he is, being with Zane is effortless. Silence or conversation, it's a feeling of contentment with him. Although there are questions about him looming in the back of my mind, today has turned out to be one of the most comfortable and peaceful days I've had in a very long time. We make small talk along the way. He asks about my students at school, and we talk a little about the bar and what a good friend Sam has been to him.

The more we walk and talk, the more I battle with myself and my thoughts of what Zane and I could be. He's closed off and that worries me. But, I guess, in some ways. I've been like that too, so I tell myself to overlook all that, and just be in the moment. Whatever happens, will happen. I just feel like I could use some good in my life for a change.

Toward the end of our walk, Zane turns to face me, his hand coming up to my face and his thumb moving across my cheek. It takes me a second...or ten...to catch my breath at his touch.

And there's the smile I can never get enough of. "How about we get some things at the farmer's market and head to my place to fix some lunch. That muffin lasted all of about a half hour. I'm starved."

"Perfect," I say with a smile. Together, we head toward the open market. I love supporting this one in particular. They've teamed up with local families from the elementary school where I work, to provide them with fresh food and food education. It's a great project, and one that is really needed.

As we get closer, we can hear the live music and can see one of the local storytellers in action as he captivates the kids with stories of long ago. The looks on the kids' faces is pure excitement; I see that look often when I read my favorite stories to my students. Nothing in the world like it. First graders are definitely my people.

The closer we get to the market, the more I think about this wonderful small town that's beginning to feel more and more like home, after moving forty-five minutes away from Raleigh. Moving from the memories, from the only home I'd ever known. Far enough away to try and forget the horrifying accident, but close enough that I can drive to the cemetery when I feel I need to.

I stop myself from lingering on those thoughts for too long. I'm having a wonderful day and I don't want to mar it with bad memories.

We choose some delicious looking fresh produce and other goodies, as Zane has promised to cook up something wonderful. It surprises me that he cooks. Never judge a book by its cover, I guess. To satisfy my sweet tooth, I choose a homemade pumpkin pie that I'm sure will taste as delectable as it looks.

We get back to our cars and decide I'll just follow Zane to his place and, once again, it astonishes me when he tells me he lives in an apartment just a block away from mine. I wonder how I never ran into him before. Hillsborough really isn't that big.

Chapter Nine

ZANE

I keep digging in deeper and deeper. How can I possibly think it's even remotely okay to bring Raina back to my apartment? I really can't seem to help myself. I'm a weak fucker.

I keep an eye on Raina in the car behind me as we pull into the lot beside the apartment building. She gets out of her car as I exit mine, with a bounce in her step that I'm not sure I've ever seen. For whatever reason, she seems happy with me, and the irony of that is not lost on me.

We make our way into my apartment, hang up our coats, and drop our bags on the counter. Raina turns to me and I see her smile. I'm lost in it. I can't take it any longer.

Almost instantly, I'm right in front of her, my hands on her hips. I can't stop. I can't keep my hands off her. Her scent is like summer rain and lavender, so sensual, so intoxicating. I lean into her, my hands in her hair, and she looks up at me, as if she's wondering what brought on the sudden change.

I look at her, study her, visibly torn between what is easy and what is right. Then I decide I don't care anymore, at least not in this moment.

"Fuck it," I growl, and then I kiss her, perhaps too frantically. Her mouth meets mine in surprise, and she opens hesitantly to let me in. Our tongues connect for the first time and her taste is like heaven. I pull her closer to me, more roughly than I'd like, but I just can't get enough of her mouth, her taste. I guide her back against the counter, and her soft hands run up and down under my shirt, nearly causing me to explode right in my jeans. This is not good, but so good, all at the same time.

My hands make their way under her shirt and I get my first touch of the softest, most delicate skin I've ever felt, and her breathing accelerates. "God, you're beautiful. The softest skin. Baby, it's gonna feel so good against mine. I'm gonna ravish you, Raina."

"Please, Zane." Her moan erupts against my lips. What a magnificent sound.

My kisses continue to rain down on her like a Midwest summer storm. Moans and whimpers fill the quiet space of my apartment. Her hips rub against me, making me harder than I've ever been in my life. My mouth devours hers, then moves to her neck. My hands find the hem of her shirt, quickly lifting it up over her head, and she suddenly stills. Her breathing is erratic, and the look on her beautiful face has apprehension written all over it.

I stop immediately. I can sense her hesitation, and my need to make her feel safe and comfortable takes over. "Jesus. I'm sorry. I got carried away."

That's putting it mildly, asshole.

I keep a hold of her but give her some room to move.

"It's okay. I just...I just want you to know something." She looks all around the room, barely making eye contact with me. Shit, she's nervous. She lowers her head and I fucking hate that. "I've never felt like this before. I thought I did, but it wasn't like this at all. I've never been with anyone like this

39

before. This....intimate." Pink makes its way from her neck clear up her gorgeous face.

She's a virgin. How did I miss this? Raina was about to give herself to me, I can feel it. And I'm the least worthy man on the planet to receive this gift. This gives a whole new meaning to *what the fuck?*

"God, I'm sorry. I wasn't thinking...I didn't know." My hand gently caresses her soft skin, trying to will away the feelings of uneasiness she's having right now, and her body relaxes slightly.

"No, no. It's...I'm okay. I just need to slow down a bit. I want this with you, I do. Just, maybe not so soon." She's staring at me, then she begins looking all around, seemingly embarrassed. "I feel so many things with you. I feel alive and genuinely happy for the first time in what seems like forever, even though you're quite serious at times," she says, smiling. "You make me feel that way. One day with you and I feel a little lighter, calmer. Like I'm living again."

Jesus, she's killing me. I can't believe this. She's like an angel.

"We'll slow down. If that's what you need, then that's what we'll do." I shake away the lustful thoughts that are filling my head and will my cock to soften a bit. Good luck with that, right?

As difficult as it is, my hands pull her shirt back down over that white lacey bra. Such a shame to cover that up; however, we're taking this slow. She deserves that. Hell, that's the very least she deserves. Not some Neanderthal like me jumping her the first chance I get. And sadly, all I can think right at this moment is the image of her panties being the same sexy white lace too.

I'm going to hell.

I pull her into me and she tucks her head under my chin,

her hands landing at my sides. I close my eyes and kiss her on the forehead as she looks up at me.

I know it now. I'm not strong enough to stay away. I need her like I need air to breathe.

I was only supposed to watch over her. That's what Zander wanted. Now, after all this time, I realize I might be in love with her. What a clusterfuck!

Chapter Ten

RAINA

O f all the things I thought would happen today, Zane consuming me with that kind of kiss wasn't on the radar. A little kiss, maybe. But, Jesus, that was nearly overwhelming.

I'm trying to process these most recent events and how quickly things are moving. Zane assures me he will slow down. I know I asked for that, but then I look at the most handsome man I've ever seen, and I wonder what the hell I was thinking. Even though Sarah doesn't quite do slow when it comes to men, and she urged me to pursue this...whatever this is, she knows I'm not her. She would have my head if she found out I did anything irrational.

Zane and I sit at the small dinette type table and chairs, eating a delicious grilled chicken salad. Turns out, Zane is an awesome cook. When he pours us both a glass of water, I wonder briefly why a man who tends bar for a living doesn't have a fridge full of beer. Come to think of it, I've never seen him drink a beer, or any alcoholic drink, for that matter.

My train of thought is broken by his deep voice. "What's

going on in that mind? It's working a mile a minute, I can tell."

"Just wondering. I don't think I've ever seen you drink before. Alcohol I mean."

He stops eating and puts down his fork. The silence lingers for a moment. "My father is an alcoholic. My brother drank a lot too. I don't want any part of that because I saw what it did to them. Kind of odd that I serve it to others, I guess. But, it's a job and it pays the rent."

"I can understand that."

He picks up his fork and continues to eat, but it's easy to see he's got a lot on his mind. He says he can tell when my mind is on the fast track. I think we're both quite perceptive people then. We finish our dinner in relative quiet, just making a bit of small talk. Oddly enough, I'm comfortable with that.

"You are truly an amazing cook. This was fantastic."

"One of my many talents," he says laughing along with me.

Feeling the need to not overstay my welcome, I start clearing my empty plate from the table, preparing to leave. I would most definitely rather stay and see where that kiss may lead, but I worry that if things become heated again, I may just give in to the physical desire to be with him, and right now, that isn't what I need. There's this sense that I need to get to know this man on a deeper level first, and I don't know where that comes from.

"This was wonderful, but I better get going. I've got some papers to check and plans I need to write for school. Thank you for today." Wondering if I'll get to see him again soon, I ask, "Would you like to come to my place tomorrow for dinner? My cooking isn't as bad-ass as yours," I say in reference to his earlier comment, "but I don't starve."

He grins and gets up from the table to come around and

meet me. "I'd like that. I'll be there around five if that works for you?"

"Five is great."

He grabs my coat and helps me slip it on, then takes my face in his hands and caresses my cheeks. His lips lower to mine and brush against them in the sweetest, most gentle kiss I've ever had.

With his lips only inches from mine, he whispers, "See you tomorrow, angel."

I freeze for a split second, my eyes drowning in his.

Angel.

It's difficult to pull myself together after that, but I do, barely. I turn around and head to my car, smiling from ear to ear. Listening to Zane gently laugh at my response to his kiss is a bit embarrassing.

But, this is happening. Zane and I are happening, I think, and I couldn't be more thrilled. Just a bit cautious, but thrilled nonetheless. I'm not at all certain what the strong connection is between us, but it's exhilarating.

As I pull into my parking spot next to my apartment building, I hear the ding of a text message.

LIAM: Hey teacher girl. We're playing at the pub this Friday night. How about we catch up?

It's Liam. God, Liam is a wonderful man. He's that guy any woman would be lucky to snag. But I'm just not that woman. I'm anxious to see where things go with Zane, so I can't.

RAINA: Hey. Sorry, but can't.
L: It's cool...it's also Zane, right?
R: I'm sorry. It's complicated.
L: I kinda figured. No worries, friend. Take care then.

I put my phone back in my purse and head up to my apartment, feeling bad about Liam, but knowing it was the right thing to do. I won't ever string a man along. I've experienced that feeling, and it isn't a good one. No one deserves that.

Chapter Eleven

ZANE

✤

S pending the rest of the day with a hard-on the size of fucking Texas isn't my idea of a good time. I have to work at the pub tonight, and my mind will most definitely *not* be on the customers.

About a minute before we open, I walk into the pub and see that Sam is in one pissed off mood. Just about the time I ask what crawled up his ass, in walks his soon-to-be-ex-wife from the back room. And cue the tension. Those two just need to fuck each other out of their systems. I don't think I've ever known two people more made for each other; they both have a stubborn streak a mile wide. I steer clear of them both and head behind the bar to get this place set up for a busy Saturday night.

Tonight is Tira's night to work, and I'm pretty sure I know how this will go down. It won't be good, but I need to put her in her place. Now that I've decided to make this thing work with Raina, no one will screw it up. And if anyone could manipulate this situation, it's Tira. I told her we were friends and that's all it will ever be, but this message frequently gets twisted in her flighty mind. I'll clear that right the hell up tonight. As screwed up as it is, I'm all in with Raina.

No sooner than that thought enters my mind, Tira walks in. I'm in no mood to deal with her shit so I call her over straight away.

"Hey, Zane. What's up, handsome? Please tell me we're headed home together tonight, babe?" she purrs, leaning in, trying to give me a show by pushing out her tits.

It's as though she's completely forgotten I left her here alone, so I could go home and try to fix the shit going on in my mind after seeing Raina with Liam.

I lean in and place both hands on the bar. "Tira, I've made it perfectly clear before. But get me this time...there is no going home together. Not tonight, not ever. Feel me?"

"Jesus, Zane. What's your problem?" she says, taking a step toward me.

"Leave it, Tira. Just fucking leave it." Pushing off the bar, I stand to my full height, which is somewhat intimidating, so that's exactly why I do it. "I don't need you all up in my shit. I've started seeing Raina. So, no manipulating, no jealousy, no fucking come-ons from you. Friends, and that's it. If you can't handle that, then the 'just friends' suggestion is off the table." I'm not sure how much clearer I can make myself. She needs to take this shit that I'm saying seriously. I won't have her messing things up.

"Fine. Clear as crystal. But I'm telling you, if you think for one minute Raina is the girl for you, you're in for a surprise. She's as goody-two-shoes as they come, babe. A regular Sandra Dee. So good luck with that." She chuckles as she turns to walk away.

Why does she have to be a bitch?

SATURDAY NIGHT at the bar is every bit as busy as I had antici-pated. Thank God Sam is here. We've all been run ragged, and by the time we close, I'm exhausted and ready to sleep till dinnertime tomorrow. The only thing that gets me through this hectic night is the thought of spending more time with Raina.

The drive home is uneventful, and I make my way to my apartment, ready to crash. My last thought before I fall to sleep is that beautiful smile. That should keep the nightmares away.

Chapter Twelve

RAINA

At five o'clock sharp, there's a knock at the door and my stomach turns slightly inside out. I know it's Zane, and I've been beside myself all day thinking about having him in my space. Yesterday was such a comforting feeling, but once we kissed, I knew what was going to eventually happen, and that feeling vanished into thin air.

I've called Sarah twice, which, as it turns out, was a mistake, because every time I mentioned Zane's name, she squealed. And I mean like a hungry pig squeal, although she probably wouldn't take too kindly to me comparing her to a pig. I couldn't figure out exactly what to wear, what to cook, how to act, and the list of unknowns went on until finally, she talked me down from the ledge by telling me just to be myself and let whatever happens, happen. That any man who was worth it would see me for the person I was.

I think about how much my mom would have helped me in this situation. She was always the level headed one, the one who could help me sort through my feelings. *But she's no longer here*, I think wistfully. She will never be here to guide me or offer advice about men, or clothes, or decorating my first home. She won't be around if I ever get married, or to help me search for the perfect wedding dress or choose the prettiest flowers.

Those ugly feelings begin to surface, threatening to pull me under. I turn to look at the picture of my parents and me, the one that made its home on the counter as soon as I moved into this apartment. It sits lovingly inside a colorful, butterfly picture frame. It's always been my favorite. Odd, because the lifespan of butterflies is extremely short, just like my parents'. I touch the glass and look at my mom, *really* look at her, and for whatever reason, a feeling of peacefulness comes over me. It's like she's telling me she and Dad are okay. She is taking a little bit of the weight of sadness off my shoulders, and helping me realize I will be okay too. Shaking off my melancholy mood is a little easier this time. Maybe I am moving on. Maybe things really will be better now.

I walk to the door and calmly open it. Now, can I just say that the man I see standing before me has to be the most beautiful specimen of a man I have ever been lucky enough to lay my eyes on? Mesmerizing might be the closest I could come to describing him. The five o'clock shadow only enhances his gorgeous face, and my first thought is how that would feel on the inside of my thighs. I can feel my eyes peruse his body from top to bottom as if they have a mind all their own.

When did I turn into that girl?

"See something you like?" He smirks as he slowly saunters his way into my apartment.

"Shit. Um...come in. Please. I apologize. You do look nice tonight."

"Nice?" He chuckles, raising his eyebrows. "Sweetheart, your eyes were all over me. I think you can do better than nice," he says, as his presence fills this room.

"Okay. How about egotistical?" His chuckle-turned-laugh makes me suddenly relax, and I take his coat and invite him into the kitchen area. I love the open floor plan of this apartment, which makes it look more spacious. There is a counter dividing the living area from the small, renovated kitchen. I pour us both a sweet tea and I take a seat on one of the small stools by the counter.

"So, how were things at the pub last night? Was Tira working?" I ask, immediately closing my eyes and wishing I had let that last question sit on my tongue instead of blurting it out.

Tilting his head to the side just a bit, Zane smiles and leans casually against the counter.

God, he's just...sex.

"Fine. Busier than usual, even for a Saturday night. And yes, Tira was working. I talked to her and told her, in no uncertain terms, that I wanted no part of being with her. Told her I didn't want her causing trouble now that I'm seeing you. She's had a thing for me for quite some time, but she is not the kind of person I want to spend a lot of time with. She gets too jealous and clingy. Plus, she's manipulative and she whines, which irritates the fuck out of me."

I smile. I hate the fact that he even has to be around the Wicked Witch of the West, so I love hearing this.

"That night when we came into the bar, we didn't come together. I was walking in and she called out for me to wait for her. We really are friends, although she'd rather it be with benefits."

I stand and lean on the other side of the counter and listen intently to what he says. Tira certainly made it seem as though they came together. Manipulative bitch.

"Thank you for telling me that. For being honest about her. I'll tell you now that, a while back, I was in a relationship. The only real relationship I've ever had. I thought he was the one, you know. I was young and inexperienced, and thought we really had something special."

The last memories I have of him are not good ones. He started drinking too much for my taste, and always made excuse as to why I could never meet his family. There was no rhyme or reason to what he did to me, and it's hard to explain how utterly confused I was when he left. My jaw clenches just a bit, and anger begins to creep into my voice. I can feel it.

"He took off with another woman. At least, that's what he said he was doing. I never really got the full story from him, and I never saw him again. For the longest time, I never felt like I was enough. That there was something wrong with me for him to have left like that. But, I've come to the conclusion that that was all on him. That I would find someone who would be with me for who I am, not who they want me to be."

My head drops, but before I can say another word, two of Zane's fingers come to my chin and tilt my head back up toward him. His eyes show no pity or sympathy, but genuine concern for me. This wonderful man has been hiding under a façade of anger and irritability, and that's not him at all. I'm beginning to see him, really see him.

"Don't ever look down on yourself, angel. You are more than enough. That guy was a dick to not recognize he had perfection right in front of him. And suffice it to say, I don't deserve someone half as wonderful as you, but for whatever reason, here I am. You keep your head up, understand?"

He takes my hand and leads me to the sofa to sit, where his lips slowly and gently make their way toward mine. With his hand moving to my cheek, he kisses me. It's a soft kiss, but so much is spoken at that moment. Trust is exchanged between us. Trust and respect and desire.

The kiss begins to turn somewhat frantic and with

butterflies ravaging my stomach, I move to straddle his lap. My hands grasp at his hair, but he grabs my wrists and looks longingly at me.

"Angel, when we decide to take that step, you let me take control. Trust me to take care of you, to pleasure you until you can't even take another breath from writhing underneath me. But right now, we're taking this slow. I want you, don't doubt that. I want you so much it's difficult to keep myself composed. I've thought about you under me for months now, and it's quite possibly making me a very demented man."

Zane runs his hands up along my arms then moves my hand between his legs.

Oh, my God. He's huge!

"You feel this? This is what you do to me, baby. I've had a perpetual hard-on since I first kissed you. Fuck, it's not going to be easy to go slow, but you and I will experience this together, and I'll cherish the gift you give me more than anything I've ever been given in my life. Give us some time, sweetheart. We'll get there."

The way he speaks to me makes me melt. So much so, that it's hard to focus. But I stay in the moment with him and let all those words sink in. His hand stays on my face, his thumb caressing my lips, swollen from his frenzied kiss.

"You're amazing, you know that?"

"Sweetheart, there hasn't been much amazing or good about me in a long time. But somehow you make me feel like I could be a good man again."

Breaking the seriousness of the moment, Zane's stomach growls low and long, and we both laugh at the sound.

"How about that dinner you promised?" he asks, as he lifts me off the sofa and places me on my unsteady legs.

"I hope you like pizza. I thought it would be fun to make one together. I bought the stuff today while I was running errands." Walking into the small kitchen, I turn to see he's right on my heels. "Homemade pizza is one of my all-time favorites. My mom and I..." I stop for an instant, clearing my throat, then go on. "My mom and I made homemade pizza about once a week. We tried every topping we could think of." And suddenly, my heart feels more satisfied and a little happier than it has in a long time.

Zane grins and brings the back of my hand to his mouth for a kiss.

"Then homemade pizza it is."

My mind is complete mush. Who is this man? And why don't they clone him for the rest of the female population?

Chapter Thirteen

ZANE

Over the next week, I spend more time with Raina, falling into a comfortable routine of dinner between the time when she gets home from work and when I head to the pub, as well as spending time with her at her apartment on the weekends. We talk and laugh a lot. I've also learned what binge watching Netflix is all about.

Some nights, she keeps me company, taking up a seat at the end of the bar, telling me story after story about the children she teaches. Smiling, being genuinely happy. That spark, that light in her, makes me think that maybe the world isn't as shitty as I once believed. Being near Raina is just easy and relaxing, and after all the bullshit I've endured in my lifetime, it's a good feeling. A feeling I don't take for granted.

On the nights that Raina is around, my eye is always on Tira. She glares at Raina constantly, and at some point, I'm convinced, she's going to stir up shit with my girl. And yes, she's mine.

I've never felt quite so protective of someone, not even my brother. Zander was always the more high-spirited and fearless of the two of us, which meant he was constantly finding trouble. Consequently, I was always watching out for him and inevitably bailing him out. Dad sure as shit didn't care, so it was just us two, looking out for each other. I do miss my brother, every damn day, and I hate that he wasn't strong enough to fight his demons. There are times when I'm tempted to blame myself for not seeing how troubled he was. I know I'm not responsible, but it's hard not to feel that way.

It's Friday night, and I'm expecting Raina at any time now. Liam and Cole are on stage, and I get a little nervous knowing Liam might have a thing for my angel. Hell, most guys here probably do, she's that amazing.

She walks in with her friend, Sarah, and she looks every bit as beautiful tonight as she does every time I see her. Those long, slender legs will be wrapped around me soon, and her long, silky, brown strands will be falling in waves down her back as she arches into me while I melt into her.

That perpetual hard-on I've mentioned? It's back. With a vengeance.

The girls sit at the bar near the back, and holler out their drink orders, obviously giddy over something. I fix their drinks, leaning over the bar as I hand Raina's to her, and whisper in her ear. "Angel, you're seriously gonna have to stop with the skin-tight jeans and those tight tops. My dick is as hard as fucking cement. I'm not quite sure how I'll make it through my shift tonight."

"Aww, baby. I'm so sorry. How about if I take off so you can concentrate?"

God, how I love to see this light-hearted side of her. I move my lips closer to her beautifully blushed cheeks and whisper in her ear.

"That sweet ass of yours better stay planted on that barstool till closing, angel. After we get things cleaned up, you and I have a date."

"A date?" she asks, flirtatiously.

"Yep. We're headed back to my apartment. Maybe for a little late-night snack," I say to her. She looks confused and it's adorable.

"A date. At two o'clock in the morning. At your apartment. To eat food."

My hand cradles the back of her neck and gently grabs hold of her luscious brown hair so she's looking directly into my eyes. "Who said anything about eating food?" I smile when I see her eyes widen with a touch of uneasiness. I brush my lips across hers and she sighs.

I release her in an instant and turn to walk away, leaving Raina with her mouth half open, her face a stunning shade of pink, and Sarah belting out a squeal rivaled only by the swine on the nearby farm.

Fuck, this night won't be over fast enough.

Chapter Fourteen

ZANE

Lucky for me, Sarah drove Raina to the pub tonight, which means I get to take her home. Only her home isn't where we're heading. Raina is getting a bit tipsy on that white wine she loves so much so after a while, I start serving her just water. She will be in complete control of her senses tonight when we hit my apartment. And she'll be in sensory overload by the time morning comes. Or by the time *she* comes.

We leave the pub together after Sam lets me go early, telling me he has everything under control to close out himself. He knows Raina is coming home with me, and he is all too willing to help me out. His soon-to-be-ex was in tonight and I'm hoping they end up together in Sam's office at some point. Those two are still deeply in love, even I can see it, and I've thought many times that I'm not sure who is the most stubborn of the pair not to realize it.

I pull into my parking space and walk around to help Raina out. I hold her hand as we walk into my apartment, and can sense some hesitancy on her part, but I know she's ready for me. She's become more open with me and there have been times this past week when we've both been anxious to get to the next level. Being tangled up with her has kept us both on edge.

I help her out of her coat and head to the fridge for drinks. She takes a few sips of her water, then looks up at me with a beautifully bashful smile. "Thanks," she says, somewhat apprehensive.

"Hey, don't get shy on me now." I lean down and kiss her cheek.

"Just a bit nervous. I think the wine made me a bit too flirty earlier, but ..." Her hesitancy is killing me.

"Hey. There's no need to be nervous. We only go as far as you want," I say, walking slowly toward her. I guide her over to the sofa and sit, pulling her onto my lap. I want to reassure her that she makes her own choices. If she says no, then it's no. Period. "I'm not here to pressure you or coerce you into anything. That's not my style. We're taking it slow, remember? That means you set the pace."

"You said you were in control when we...you know. What does that mean to you?"

"It means when you're ready for me, I'll have you and I decide what we do, and where. I lead, and you just let yourself feel. If I do something you don't want, then you tell me, and I stop. Does that make sense?"

Raina's hand comes to my face, and I feel her nervousness begin to calm. She leans in and kisses me with all the trust in the world. "Yes. It does." Right at this moment, I accept that she's mine now to protect, to take care of. From the moment I laid eyes on this girl, this is what I've wanted, yet I never imagined I'd have it.

Taking her hand, I stand, gently pulling her with me, and walk her into my bedroom. We stand by the bed and both my hands move tenderly, caressing her face. I can feel the heat, and see her flushed cheeks, as my hands gently make their way into her hair. *Slow*, I remind myself.

Right now, she's exposing her emotions through those sparkling, expressive eyes of hers, and they're telling a story. She wants to be mine.

My favorite kind of story.

My lips connect with hers gently. Bar none, this has to be the most gratifying kiss I've ever had the pleasure of giving and experiencing. It's not forceful or uncontrolled, but sensual. Damn if it won't be hard to keep this at a slow pace.

I move my hands from her hair to her waist and teasingly pull her shirt over her head, dropping it to the floor. Her jeans are next and land right on top of the shirt. With any luck, they'll still be on the floor in the morning.

She's an absolute vision, an angel on Earth. I unequivocally do not deserve this, or her, but here she is nonetheless. And the undeniable chemistry between the two of us only fuels the fire I have for her.

I lay her down on my bed and step back to remove my clothes, which land in a jumbled heap right beside hers. She looks at me and I see her confidence growing. Her small hands run down my muscled abs that I work so hard to maintain, her fingers shaking ever so slightly as she touches me. But I know she wants me as badly as I want her. Every nerve in my body awakens to her touch.

With all the courage she can muster, she pulls her hands away from me and reaches back to unhook her bra, taking it off completely and tossing it across the bed. Her cheeks turn pink, but I see a smile hinting at her luscious lips. She lays back on the bed with only her panties between me and paradise.

"You have no idea what you do to me, do you?"

She shakes her head slowly.

Running my hands along her thighs, I feel her shiver. My

fingers inch closer to the heat between her legs, and I can't take it anymore. This is so much better than I could have ever imagined it would be. She is, without a doubt, the most intoxicating woman, and the depraved thoughts running through my mind right now would most likely send her running.

Dancing around this beauty, trying to avoid interacting too much with her, has been a test of my fucking patience. But, she's here now. So without hesitation, I slide her white, lacy panties down over her gorgeous, toned thighs. She tenses slightly, her reaction subtle, but clear. I slow down and smile, giving her some reassurance.

My boxer briefs come off next, and I lean over her to kiss her softly. I use the tip of my tongue to lick the perimeter of her lips and I can feel her breath hitch as I do. I am so rock-fucking-hard right now that I can barely hold back. This slow, gentle seduction has me teetering on the edge, and I'm just about to fall over head-first and crash land.

As I continue to kiss her, my hands wander over her luscious skin, learning every nuance of her body, which causes goose bumps to rise on her arms. My lips leave hers and begin a trail down to her firm breasts where I stop for a moment, taking a taste of each one. My tongue traces her hardened nipple, my teeth gently nipping at the sensitive peak, as her head thrashes back and forth, her flesh igniting in pleasure.

I know for certain she's never had anyone make her feel like this before, which means she's in for a night of pure heaven she won't soon forget. Because this is us, together, wanting and needing each other.

Her eyes gently fall closed and a sigh escapes through her lips. "Stay with me, sweetheart," I say, trying to keep her in the moment with me.

As my mouth begins its descent down to her heated core,

I gently lick her stomach as my hands begin to massage her breasts. I can hear her breathing pick up as my fingers take their turn playing, rolling her nipples between my fingertips. Her hips move in desperation, trying to find something to help ease the ache my ministrations are causing her.

Using my shoulders to gently urge her legs apart, my tongue finally reaches its destination and I see her back arching as I take a slow, delectable lick between her legs. Her taste is magnificent. Now that I've had this, I know for certain no one else will ever compare to her sweetness.

I continue to devour her with my mouth, teasing and sucking, until I can feel the signs of an orgasm building. Her body begins to shake and her legs tremble as her hands come to my hair. She's primed and ready to fall over the edge.

"Oh God. Zane...I've never...I can't..." She screams, as she attempts to regain some control.

I hear her quivering voice, then she orgasms spectacularly. I can barely hold her still. Her knees pull up, and her stomach shakes, her back arching in sweet release, and from her throat comes the most euphoric moan I've ever heard. Raina in the midst of an orgasm is a sight to behold, one that I will have imprinted on my mind for the rest of my life. Without a doubt, she won't forget it either.

Shit, I've never seen a woman come so hard in all my life.

Her body begins to settle as my tongue licks its way back up her stomach, taking one last turn at her breasts, then up to her mouth. Her breathing finally evens out, and she sighs contentedly. My hands run through the smooth ribbons of hair, causing her eyes to close.

"My God, that was amazing," she whispers.

"That's just the beginning angel."

It is only the beginning. I can assure her of that. I'll never be able to get enough of her now.

The assault on her body continues as I swirl my fingers around her stomach, then lower to her pulsing core. I plunge two fingers inside her warm, wet heat, as I prepare her for me. I know I'm big, and because she's a virgin, I almost consider using lube, but when I reach for her, she's soaking. So ready for me.

"You are so wet, babe. Are you sure about this? This is what you want?"

"Yes. I'm sure."

I stop briefly because she needs to hear and understand this. "If you need me to slow down or stop, just say so."

She nods in agreement, her innocence overwhelming.

"Words, angel. I need to hear the words."

"I'll let you know if I need to stop. But I'm ready for you, Zane. I've never been surer of anything in my life."

Raina spreads her legs guardedly as I put on a condom. I hover over her, and guide my painfully hard cock to her opening, slipping just a bit into heaven. She closes her eyes.

"Eyes, Raina. I need your eyes, darlin'." She opens her beautiful brown eyes and so help me God, I see her soul. She's giving me this, and trusts me to take care of her.

What the hell did I ever do to deserve this?

I enter her slowly, and I can feel the barrier break. I watch as Raina grimaces and squeezes her eyes shut, then opens them again, tears coming from the corners.

"God, I hate hurting you. Are you okay?"

"I'm fine. Overwhelmed, I think. But you need to move. Please move."

And with her approval, I begin to move, slowly at first. I can feel her hips rising up to meet mine, thrusting in time with my movements. Damn, I've never felt this kind of gratification during sex. It's as though her body was built just for mine, and I groan as we continue this sensual dance with each other.

My hands run up and down her body, then stop as they reach her hair. She is everything. This is everything.

Soon, our pace begins to quicken, and I'm overwhelmed with a yearning that I've never felt before. Emotions surface that I can't even quite name at this point. My mind is mush.

We're so totally absorbed in each other, and we begin moving in sync even more quickly. Her shaking legs tell me she's close to another orgasm, and I'm the lucky son-of-a-bitch that gets to be inside her to feel it.

"That's it. Give it to me. Let yourself go. I've got you, baby." I continue to move inside her, pulling her hands up over her head, controlling them and linking her fingers with mine. We've become one, and my heart bursts.

She cries out as her orgasm consumes her and I can feel her walls squeezing me. I come hard, much more quickly than I'd like, but that's what this woman does to me. I'm half off balance and totally out of control when it comes to her. And I can't think of a better way to be.

Our movements slow way down, almost coming to a complete stop. I let out an exhausted sigh and my eyes meet hers. I smile because the look I see on her face tells me all I need to know. She looks very much like one sated woman, her eyes closed and her cheeks flushed. I'm also relieved that I don't see guilt or regret. She does seem a bit reticent at the moment, but, I know she's okay; she's just emotional since this is her first time. I roll off her and pull her body in close to mine.

"Baby, you are amazing, and you are the most beautiful shade of pink right now," I say chuckling just a little.

"Zane, don't tease," she says laughingly, lightly punching my shoulder. Then her expression changes and she turns serious. "I don't think I've ever felt the way you made me feel tonight. Cherished and protected. Thank you."

"Believe me, the pleasure was mine. Let me take care of

this condom. Stay right there." I move off her and start to stand.

"Zane, I'm..."

My movements cease. "Remember when I said I'll take care of you? Well, this is me, taking care. Stay right there."

After I wrap the condom and throw it in the trash, I take a warm cloth to the bed and help Raina clean up a bit. I think she's a bit embarrassed, but when I said I'll take care of her, I meant in every way. She'll get used to it. She gives a slight gasp and winces at the sight of a little blood on the wash-cloth. Heading back to the bathroom, I toss the washcloth in the sink and hurry back to bed where I see Raina curled up under my sheet and blanket. At the sight of me, she sits up and looks around nervously.

"I'm sorry. I don't really know...should I leave or..."

"Jesus, Rain. No. You are staying right here." I move to sit beside her and tilt that face back up toward me. "What did I tell you about dropping your head? Angel, we are an 'us' now. You stay the night with me, or I stay the night with you. Doesn't matter. You do not get up to leave after I make love to you. You're in this bed with me tonight."

"I love that you call me Rain."

I move under the covers beside her and pull her close. "Me, too."

"I don't have pajamas or anything, I mean...is, um, that how you sleep?"

"Yes. And when you're in my bed, you're naked, or at least no panties. I need to have easy access," I say, smiling.

"Okay. Any other demands?" she says with a grin.

"Yes...sleep. Sleep well. Because I am nowhere near finished with you."

And I will never be.

She sighs and scoots back toward me, her back against my front, which means her ass is against my dick. Shit. I give myself five minutes and I'll be hard again. But, I consider the fact that tonight is the first for Raina, and I know I'll have to be mindful of that. She'll be sore for a while anyway.

I lay beside her, listening to her gently breathing as she falls fast asleep. The more I think about her, the harder I fall. My brother would be so pissed right now, I know it. I consider that I'm the one who constantly bailed him out, yet he's the one who bailed on life, so I'm taking something for me. It's time for me to have what I want. And I want her. Raina is mine.

Her breathing deepens, and her warm body snuggles closer in to me, causing my heart and my head to calm a little.

After all that thinking, I'm left wondering when in the hell I became the guy that snuggles after sex.

Chapter Fifteen

I can't breathe. My mom and dad. They're standing on the other side of the road, covered in blood, reaching for me, holding on to each other. I can't get to them! Why can't I move? I reach out my arms, but suddenly they disappear.

I'm frantic, wiping my eyes and looking more closely. There's a police officer standing where they stood. He begins walking towards me. He says they're gone.

"But they just went out for a walk. They should be back. Where are they?"

"I'm sorry, but they're dead," the officer tells me. I fall to my knees and let out a scream that comes from the absolute depths of my soul. I'm alone, all alone. They're gone and when they left, I wasn't even here to say goodbye. I cry out to God and ask why He took them from me.

"Why?!" I scream and scream louder. It can't be...

"Raina." I hear the officer call.

"Raina!" he calls again.

"Angel! Wake up!" another voice beckons.

I sit straight up in bed, looking all around, almost dripping with sweat. I try shaking off the images from the nightmare, but they'll be ingrained in my mind for the rest of the day, I just know it..

"Rain, what the hell? Are you okay?" It's Zane, and by the look on his face, I've scared him half to death. The only one more scared than him is obviously me.

"Um...yeah, I'm good," I say, trying to shake the horrible images from my mind. "I had...I had a nightmare. I'm okay."

Zane is still holding onto me as I attempt to wiggle away, but his grip stays firm and I can't go anywhere. My heart is still racing and my breathing is still heavy. I can't believe I had this nightmare. I haven't dreamed of my parents' death for months. Why are the dreams back all of a sudden?

I take several deep breaths, in through my nose and out my mouth, calming myself.

"Tell me what's wrong," Zane demands. "You were thrashing around in bed and screaming out the word 'why' over and over. What was that dream about?" He looks worried. He wants to help me, and I consider that for a moment. I know he is struggling with his own issues, so I'm not sure I want to burden him with mine.

Although, maybe talking about my parents to him might help. Just talk in general about the accident, and leave out all the details. Maybe, talk about it some and hopefully, the dreams won't come back. I never really talked about it to anyone, except Sarah. I guess maybe Zane should know the truth about them anyway so I mentally prepare myself to share the most horrific moment of my life with this man. He is so much of a protector that I know he'll understand. I've always hesitated to talk about my parent's accident. Too many memories I'd just rather not relive.

I grab Zane's tee shirt from the floor and pull it over my head. I sit up and begin to share the story of losing the two most important people in my life.

"A few years back, my mom and dad were killed in an

accident. A drunk driver ran up onto the sidewalk where they were walking one evening. It was late, and whoever was driving just ran them over." I take a few deep breaths in and let it out hoping to hold off the tears, but they begin to fall anyway.

"Whoever it was fled the scene and since there was no one else..." I hiccup and try to get my mind focused and my voice back in control. "No one else was around, so he, or maybe she, was never found. I don't know who killed my mom and my dad. One minute, they were alive and well and happy, and the next, they were gone. I'm still confused and I'm angry." My voice begins getting a bit louder and the tears are falling faster than I can wipe them away. My heart is being torn apart again. I try concentrated breathing again, but I'm shaking and the breathing isn't helping.

Zane continues to hold me, and I can feel his body shudder with what seems like anger. I lean on him for comfort. "They're gone. They were here one night, and the next night, they were gone forever...just gone. God, Zane, I'm so sorry. I can't do this...I'm not strong..."

"Yes. yes, you are. You don't have to say anything else. God, baby, you're shaking so bad. Shhh...I've got you. I'll always have you."

I look up to see Zane fighting back tears. This strong, commanding man, this man I'm clinging to in desperation, is in tears over my loss. And I feel every one of them to the depths of my soul.

His lips gently land on my forehead. He leaves them there, and holds me tightly, as I continue to cry into his chest. I cry for my parents who will never know Zane and how wonderful he is to me. I cry for me and for all the milestones in my life they will not be a part of. I just cry. Even with Zane holding onto me, I feel so alone.

"There's no family left for me. They were taken away

from me, and I have to live with that for the rest of my life." I hold onto Zane like a lifeline as he rocks me back and forth.

Eventually, I pull back. My eyes find his, and for a moment, a look of...guilt flashes in his eyes. I can't understand what I see, and it confuses me. He looks away, then pulls me back in to comfort me.

"Zane? What..."

"Shhh...just sit with me. Let me take care of you."

We sit like that for a long time, the strange look in his eyes moments ago forgotten, until finally, I let the darkness take over and allow myself to fall asleep, where I don't have to think about how alone I am.

❦

I WAKE to find myself alone in Zane's bed, still in his t-shirt and wrapped in his blanket and comforter. I roll over and discover cold sheets where he had slept. I cover my eyes with my arm and listen for any sound of life outside of the bedroom. I completely broke down in front of Zane and he will no doubt cut me loose after that display of crazy. No one signs up for that.

I look around the room and locate my clothes from last evening. I get up and head for the bathroom to tame what can only be a rat's nest on my head. I'm sure my eyes are rimmed in red and the pink splotches most likely covering my face will make for a dazzling appearance, most definitely.

Looking into the mirror, I find the assessment of my image to be spot on. I look like hell. After washing my face, picking through my hair with my fingers to tame it as best I can, and using my finger as a toothbrush, I emerge from the bathroom to find Zane sitting on the bed with two cups of coffee. He went out to get me coffee. God, this man.

"Good morning. Or good afternoon, I should say. You

slept late." He looks as handsome as ever sitting there in his jeans and Sam's Pub tee. He's a bit solemn and even worried, judging by the expression on his face, but still unbelievably handsome.

"Hey. I thought you didn't like coffee," I say jokingly, as I move towards the bed.

"Oh, it tastes like shit, no doubt. But you love it, so I can, I don't know, acquire the taste maybe?" He makes me laugh. "I know what's going through that mind right now. I'm not going anywhere, gorgeous."

With that, Zane puts the coffees on the nightstand and saunters over to me. His hands reach my waist and he pulls me closer, taking a good long look at me, from my toes clear up to the disorderly looking mess on top of my head, and giving me a wink when he finishes ogling me.

At least my breath smells somewhat pleasant.

"You should wear my shirts all the time. Without a bra. And of course, no panties."

"So, last night's unveiling of my crazy hasn't tempted you to kick me out? Because I can guarantee anyone else, except for maybe Sarah, would have bailed on me."

"Well, then aren't you lucky I'm not just anyone else. I told you last night I was here for you. Those weren't empty words. I am here. To help in any way I can. However long it takes to get through this, I'm with you. And I'm counting on being with you long after you've worked through it all."

"What if I never really get over it?"

Zane takes my hand and pulls me over to where we're both sitting on the bed. He turns to face me, never letting it go.

"Sweetheart, you will never forget your parents. They were your life for twenty-two years. So you don't just 'get over it'. Your past has been hard. But, baby, that's what makes you strong. It's been years, and I know you feel, in some ways, like the accident happened just yesterday. You've survived, and you've done amazing things with your life so far. We're going to find a way to help you move on from all this hurt. And one day, remembering won't be so bad."

Zane reaches out and with his thumb, brushes my tears away.

"No more tears today. Have faith, angel. You'll get there."

He speaks to me with such sincerity and such conviction, that it's almost overwhelming. I thought when I looked at my mom and dad's picture earlier in the week that I was getting better, feeling more settled, like things were taking a turn for the better. However, rehashing their deaths has made me second guess that. But with Zane's encouragement, maybe the light at the end of the tunnel is closer than I imagine. Maybe I wasn't left here alone after all. Maybe he came into my life for a reason.

And I'm so glad he did.

Chapter Sixteen

ZANE

I am well and truly fucked. I keep saying that, and yet I ignore every single warning sign. When she woke from that nightmare in tears, it nearly broke me. And I felt every one of those tears down to the absolute depths of my soul. I knew she was dreaming of the accident, and it was all I could do to hold myself together while I watched her fall apart. Jesus, I feel like a monster.

I'm creating a disaster of the most epic proportions and I am incapable of stopping it. I had Raina for one night, and one night will never be enough. Our coming together was like throwing a lit match into a tank of gasoline, and the explosion was magnificent. Tragic, but magnificent, because this can only end one way.

But it won't end unless she finds out. The only other person who knows is my dad, and since dear old dad is a total screw-up, as well as a raging alcoholic, he probably doesn't even remember. The question is, how long I can live with the guilt? Those same feelings, for all intents and purposes, ended my brother's life.

I'm keeping her safe and helping her move on, helping her cope, right? That certainly counts for something.

I try reasoning with myself, but my brain screams back at me.

You're lying to her, that's not helping her at all.

Damn it, I have got to get this shit under control. Like, yesterday.

❧

I TAKE Raina to her apartment for a quick change of clothes and we head out.

We make our way into the coffee shop, and sit down at the same cozy table where we met for coffee over a week ago, although some days, it feels as though I've known her forever. The same annoying waitress makes her way to our table, much less confident than last time. I think she got my message loud and clear that I wasn't the least bit interested. She takes our order and leaves promptly, keeping her eyes off me the entire time.

I reach over to snag Raina's hand as she looks out the front window. I remember looking through the window at her sitting there as I was coming into the shop to meet her that first time. Even though this time she looks a bit more reserved, she's still beautiful. I know what's going through her mind, and she's too worried about what I'm thinking, so I smile at her reassuringly.

I'm trying to keep the guilt at bay while I sit here with her and contemplate how I can just push all this shit to the back of my mind. It's the only way for me to move on with her. Forget about the past. It's over and done with, and there is fuck all I can do to change it. What I can change, though, is Raina. I'll help her learn to make her new normal without her parents, but here with me in Hillsborough. I can do that. At this point, it's really all I want.

The coffee and pastries we order are served up within a few minutes and just as I thought, the coffee is shit. But it's beginning to grow on me. I guess it really is an acquired taste. I just load it up with creamer and sugar, which helps considerably.

"Penny for your thoughts." Raina leans over and whispers, "You look like the wheels are churning a mile a minute in that head of yours."

I take a deep breath. "I'm wondering how I got to be the lucky bastard that gets to sit with you and consume a cup of the most shit-tasting beverage I've ever had to pleasure to indulge in. And I mean that with the most sincerity I can muster."

Raina throws back her head and laughs, and it's breath-taking. The trash clogging up my thoughts is instantly gone, watching her genuine laughter.

"What do you want to do today? It's kinda cold out, but if you want to hit the Riverwalk, I'm in." I've got something serious to ask her and I'm trying to figure out the right time to do it. Nervous is a feeling I'm not comfortable with, so I just want to get it over with.

"Nah. Too cold. How about we take a ride? Just get in the car and go."

"Well then, what are we waiting for?"

We quickly finish our pastries and take our coffees to go, heading out to the car that I consider my pride and joy. It feels so good to have Raina riding along with me. She looks comfortable in the passenger seat, like she's always belonged here.

I start to drive, heading west. We eventually merge onto I-40, heading toward Winston-Salem.

Raina talks a lot about her life growing up in Raleigh as I

drive. She tells me about why she decided to become a teacher and her time in college. When she shares that she graduated with honors, I'm not surprised. Along with her many other admirable qualities, she also very smart.

I reach over and lay my hand on her leg, moving my thumb up and down the outer part of her thigh. As the movements continue, I can hear a hitch in Raina's breath. I affect her just as much as she affects me, and I have a feeling our chemistry will only intensify with time.

I feel relieved that she seems to be content talking to me and sharing some memories of her youth. There are times during our conversation when her heart seems a little lighter, and I even see a determined smile on her pretty face, like she's acknowledging her feelings and is beginning to realize that remembering may truly be a good way to heal. Perhaps the slight breakdown last night was cathartic for her. Maybe that was the breaking point and from this time forward her emotions will be easier to handle. For her sake, I pray that's the truth.

"What made you decide to become a bartender?" Raina asks, interrupting the silence. I think about the answer to that question. I kept my eye on her while she still lived in Raleigh and when I discovered she was moving, I discreetly talked with the moving company to find out what city was on her radar. Shortly after, I moved as well. I didn't even think twice. Perhaps there's always be a pull toward her.

God, that makes me sound like a damn stalker.

I figured out she and her friend Sarah frequented Sam's Pub on the weekends, so I thought that would be a good place to keep tabs on her. They were hiring a bartender, and it was a stroke of luck that I found a job that quickly. But I certainly can't tell her that fucked up story.

I look over to Raina and shrug my shoulder. "I don't really know. I needed work and Sam was hiring. Since that's where I first saw you, I guess I could say it was a good move on my part." She quickly agrees. "Where did you live before Hillsborough?"

That question causes my hands to tense on the wheel. Raleigh is big, right? There are over 400,000 people who live there. So, it stands to reason I would have never met her before. At least I can be truthful about my former home.

"I lived around the Raleigh area most of my life. It's a nice city, gets bigger all the time. Lots of young people, even families, moving into the area."

"Wow. We lived in the same place and never ever crossed paths. Of course, it's such a big place, it's no wonder," she says looking out the window at the scenery passing by.

"Yeah," is about the only way I can respond, guilt weighing on my mind.

I need to change the direction of this conversation. "We're getting close to Winston-Salem. How about if we find a something good to eat?"

Raina glances at me, a mischievous look on her face. "The last time you told me we were eating, you said it wouldn't be food. So, I'm not at all sure how to answer that, handsome." I can't help but laugh. It's when she calls me handsome that I can tell she is definitely getting more comfortable with me, and a bit more confident. I love it.

"You are most definitely right about that. And last night's cuisine was, simply put, the most delectable meal I'd ever tasted. But right now, I'm damn hungry for real food." I look over to find those cheeks glowing pink again and her hands fidgeting in her lap. Her inexperience with sex makes her naïve in some ways, which is a contradiction to the snarky 'handsome' comment a moment ago.

Last night with her, taking her innocence the way I did, is a night I will keep locked away in the small, nearly empty treasure chest in my mind. Few experiences in my life have been good enough to hold onto as memories, which I find achingly unfortunate. My brother, and now Raina, are the two good things God has blessed me with. They are my treasures. In a way I guess I never realized how important Raina would become to me, and now I can't imagine a life without her in it.

§.

A FEW MORE MILES PASS, and I pull off the interstate into the parking lot of an Italian restaurant. Just as I put the car in park, I hear the most dick-hardening moan coming from the passenger seat. And it worked. I'm hard.

I slam my head back on the headrest. "Jesus, Raina. Can you not moan like that?"

"Oh, my God. I'm sorry. I just love Italian. I can already smell it out here in the parking lot." Her hands come up to cover her eyes, but they can't hide the blush that starts at her neck and makes its way slowly up to her deep brown eyes.

"Next time, we'll just hit up a burger joint. The aroma isn't nearly as potent. That way you can keep those fucking moans to yourself," I say jokingly.

I get out of the car and quickly move to the passenger side, opening the door for her. A real gentleman move, if you ask me. I take her hand and we enter the restaurant. This is a marvelous, unpretentious little place, with small tables covered in red and white checked tablecloths, and unscented candles scattered around, giving the place a romantic feel.

We're seated quickly and order our food. The Italian smells are definitely overwhelming here and I feel like moaning myself.

As I look over at Raina, I see happiness dancing in her eyes, and that makes me smile because I'm the one who put that happiness there. Now's the time to summon up some courage and just ask her what I've been considering for a few days now.

"So, I was thinking. Your winter break is coming up. There's the fact that I don't really speak to my family at all and, well, with your situation..." I see a slightly pained look on her face, and I reach to grab her hand for comfort and support. "I guess what I'm trying to say is, I'd like to spend the holiday doing something with you. We can do whatever you want. We can hang in town, or go somewhere together. Maybe the beach. I can ask Sam for a few days off. What do you say?"

Raina doesn't even hesitate. "I'd say that sounds like a great idea. And I think the beach sounds heavenly. I always loved going to the beach with my parents. There's something so soothing about sitting on the balcony in the evening and listening to the waves crashing on the sand, over and over." She stops for a second. "Sometimes I wish the waves could just sweep all my troubles out to sea."

In my mind, Raina *is* like the ocean. She is beautiful on the surface, but underneath, there is a magnificence that remains hidden. But I see it. I see her. I see my angel, and I know she is mine.

Chapter Seventeen

RAINA

J ust thinking about the trip to the beach with Zane has my mind in overdrive. It's exciting to think about, but since I haven't been there since my parents passed, it may be an emotional few days. For now, I'll just enjoy my time here today, and put the thoughts of my parents on the back burner.

As we sit here, indulging on this Italian deliciousness, I try not to let another embarrassing moan pass my lips, but it's so difficult, considering this is just about the best tasting, most mouth-watering food I've ever had. The little restaurant we found is amazing. The owners and wait-staff are obviously one-hundred percent Italian, considering their accent is so heavy. I'm enjoying the atmosphere here as well as the food and, of course, the company.

Zane and I talk about the kinds of food we enjoy most, and I learn that he definitely has a sweet tooth, which, by looking at those marvelously carved abs, you'd never guess. I love getting to know more about him. I share with him about my friendship with Sarah, and I learn that Zane's only real friend is Sam at the bar. When I ask about his brother, he becomes withdrawn, which leads me to believe there is no relationship there at all. I wonder how this man has been affected by his upbringing, as I know it wasn't good. I'd love to know more, but I'd rather it be on his terms, in his own time. Family questions seem to torment him, and I don't want to spoil this day being together. I know from experience that people come to terms with hardships in their own way. I'd love to be able to help him, though...just like he is helping me.

We finish our meal and walk back to the car hand in hand, utterly stuffed from the pasta. Zane's touch still affects me and causes me to pause for just a moment when he reaches for me.

Deciding to head back toward home, we get in the car and we're on our way.

"We can go to my place once we get back, if you'd like. Sam's wife, well almost ex-wife, is helping at the bar tonight, which should be a real shitstorm, by the way, so I'm off. We could watch a movie or something."

Feeling a little brave, I say, "How about the 'or something'?"

I can hear Zane's muffled groan, and I giggle, *actually giggle*, at the way he is affected by me. Me, of all people. I still can't get over what a man like Zane sees in someone like me. Sarah keeps telling me I'm a catch, so maybe there's more there than what I see.

"Then 'or something' it is." He reaches over, running his hand all the way up my thigh, and brushes against my center, causing me to gasp. When I glance over at him, the look on his face is determination and lust and need all mixed together. I have this feeling I'm in for one hell of a ride when we hit his apartment. And I can't wait.

It's dark by the time we make it back to Zane's place. When we hit the door to his apartment, he's at his breaking point, I can tell, because he nearly drags me inside and slams the door shut with his foot.

Good God, that was hot.

He stops briefly, lets out a breath, and pulls me close to him, his hands running up and down my back. His tongue licks along the seam of my lips and separates them, so it can make its way into my mouth. He kisses me slowly, his tongue dancing with mine. What I thought would be a frantic, no-holds-barred kiss becomes slower and more sensual. It's taken me by surprise, but I certainly don't complain. His kiss stirs up my emotions and my insides heat up with the feel of it. I could live on Zane's kisses.

"Are you okay? To do this again?" he asks, wanting reassurance from me that I'm physically ready for him again. And believe me, I am definitely ready.

"Yeah, I'm good. I'd really like a shower first, if that's okay. I didn't get one this morning, and I feel kind of icky."

He laughs. "Icky? Sweetheart, you couldn't be icky if you rolled around in mud and sat in it all day. Let's get you a shower then."

"Um, so we're going to, you know, shower together?" I ask, as he pulls me toward the bathroom. These experiences are so new to me. I've done my share of reading romance novels, but to experience it first-hand is unfamiliar.

"Figure it's a good way to save water. Better for the planet and all," he says with half a grin, his eyebrows dancing up and down as he pulls me toward the bathroom. Even half a grin on this man is sexy.

"Okay, for the good of the planet then."

Zane turns on the water to the oversized shower. I know what is going to happen in there, and it has nothing to do with getting clean. He takes my hand and guides me in, the streams of warm water from the huge showerhead above running down my body. Zane leans over, cups my face with both hands, and tilts my head back to let the warm water run through my hair and cascade down my back. He grabs shampoo from the ledge, lathers it in his hands, and begins to wash my hair. So help me, this has to be the most sensual, most intimate, feeling I've ever known. I have never felt so cared for, so protected in my life. His hands run slowly through my hair, causing my eyes to close. My body is awakened to the feelings he brings out in me.

I can feel how hard he is as I lean into him, and the most wonderful thing is that he is taking care of me first. He runs conditioner through my hair then lathers up soap to wash my body. My back is to his front, his hands are everywhere. Over my shoulders, swirling down to my breasts, my stomach, and when he reaches between my legs, I can almost feel them give way as I struggle to stay standing. The onslaught of emotions is overwhelming, the circuits running through my body firing off continuously. He runs his fingers along my overly-stimulated center, and I can barely breathe.

Zane leans in so close to me and whispers, "You have no idea how beautiful you are, do you? I love making you feel good, making you want me like this. So turned on." His hands are still caressing me, so provocatively. The way he talks to me when we're like this is exhilarating. So much so, that I'm unable to respond to his voice. And, again, within seconds, my legs nearly give out.

"Babe, you okay?" he asks, holding me up.

"Oh, God. So good. No one's ever taken care of me like this before."

"I'll always take care of you, sweetheart." He turns me to face him, showing me warmth in his eyes. It's almost frightening in a way what I feel for this man in such a short amount of time.

"Can I wash you too?"

Zane opens his arms and smiles. "As dirty as you made me last night, darlin', you better get to work."

And so I do. I wash him as gently and lovingly as he did me. My hands run over his body, which, to me, looks like a work of art.

Once he is rinsed off, I gather up all the courage I can and begin to kneel on the floor of the shower. His eyes widen in surprise. "Sweetheart, you don't have to do this."

"I want to. Tell me what you like," I say, as I take him in my hands and begin to move slowly from the base to the tip, using the soap to make him slick. He leans his head back against the tile and groans loudly. I feel powerful that I can do this to him, make him feel this way. It's excitement I've only ever imagined.

"Rinse off the soap and take me in your mouth, angel." I do as I'm told, and wrap my lips around his length. Tentatively, I dart out my tongue, swirling around the head. "God, just like that. Just like that."

Zane is so big that I keep my hand at the base and guide him in as far as I can. This experience is so new to me, but I love making him feel good. My head bobs back and forth as my hand massages the rest of him. His legs shake with pleasure and his hands are on the sides of my head, guiding me along.

Within a few minutes' time, I feel his hands move quickly under my arms, and he pulls me up to him.

At the risk of being embarrassed that he doesn't want me to finish, my head lowers and I, for a moment, feel inadequate, that this wasn't good enough for him. But then I remember how he responded to my mouth on him, his reaction and his moans of delight, and it gives me a sense of confidence. I look up to see him settling his eyes on me.

"There's my girl. Baby, when I come - and if you'd gone

on about ten more seconds, I would have - I want to be inside you. Let me get you dried off and we'll take this to the bed."

After stepping out of the shower, he gently dries me off and squeezes the excess water out of my hair. Within seconds, I'm lifted up and carried to his bed, where he obliterates every ounce of self-doubt in my mind. He is intoxicating and passionate. It's ecstasy. I don't think I'll ever get enough of this man.

After hours of kissing, and exploring, and intimacy, he snuggles in and holds me as we lay together, my head tucked comfortably under his chin for the rest of the night.

Chapter Eighteen

ZANE

❧

I'm finally beginning to feel more content and comfortable as I navigate this relationship with Raina. We continue to see each other as often as possible. She spends time with Sarah, however, while I'm at work. It's important to me that she stays close with Sarah. Those two have a wonderful relationship and she needs Sarah in her life. I can't say I was too unhappy, though, to see Liam talking with Sarah one evening when I had Raina held hostage at the bar with me. That puts my mind a little more at ease.

In all honesty, there really wasn't much of a choice when it came to Raina, though. From the moment I first saw her, there was an attraction to this girl that ran far deeper than just the physical. She is everything good in the shitty world I've lived in for years. Even in her despair, I see so much love inside her. I believe that's what makes her good at her job too. She genuinely cares about people, especially her students.

We're getting ready to head to the coast for a few days over her Christmas break. Sam closes the pub for a few days at Christmastime, so this short reprieve from bartending is perfect. I'm thankful for that, and for the extra day he gave me to take Raina away. I've been stashing away most all the money I make after I pay my rent. It isn't much, but when added to the small fund from my grandparents, who passed away years ago, I'm doing just fine.

We decide to head to Wrightsville Beach. We were able to secure an oceanfront beach house that I know will be perfect. I'm excited to give Raina the small Christmas gift I bought for her. She'll understand the significance of it, and I'm hoping it's another message to her that moving on is okay, but so is remembering.

Raina meets me at the door of her apartment, bouncing on her toes, and offers me a huge smile. I take her bags and stow them in the trunk with mine. Jokingly, I told her she didn't need clothes at all, and I find it endearing that those kinds of comments still make her blush a bit.

It takes over two hours to drive to Wrightsville and in that time, we talk, we laugh, and Raina even belts out a Grammy-worthy version of her favorite song. The sun is bright in the sky and it warms the inside of the car as we make our way east. We are so comfortable with each other now and I couldn't be happier.

We hit the drive-thru for a milkshake for me, and some flavored iced coffee with whipped cream thing for her. Now I'm wondering why the hell I didn't pack some of that cream stuff to lick off her delectable body at some point during our vacation. I look over at her smiling face and see a dab of left-over cream on the corner of her mouth. My thumb reaches over to steal it away before she can lick it, and I bring it to my mouth, sucking it in and imagining what I shouldn't be while driving. Raina closes her eyes, and I know, sure as shit, she's thinking the same thing I am.

Yep, rock hard, again..

Arriving at our beach house brings an uncertain and

tentative smile to Raina's face. I know she is reliving memories from her trips to the beach with her parents. Her loss is one I can't truly identify with. If I were to find out my parents had died, it would bother me, but wouldn't be a heartbreaking loss like it is for her. Sad, but true.

I reach over to take her hand in mine, in a silent show of support. She squeezes tightly, almost as tightly as she squeezes her eyes shut, and I am shattered to see a tear fall from the corner of her closed eye. Right this moment, I'm rethinking this entire plan.

"We don't have to stay. Whatever you want, babe."

She takes in a deep, cleansing breath in and lets it out more confidently. She looks at me and I'm lost in her. I'm ready to give this girl the fucking moon if she asks. It's in that very moment, the moment she looks at me with all the hope in the world, that I know I love her. I love her with an intensity I didn't know I possessed.

"You know what...I'm good. It's overwhelming, being here without them, but with you right here, I'm okay. I'm happy, really happy, for the first time in years. We're staying, and I'll remember, and I'll be okay."

I love her.

THE BEACH HOUSE is the comfortable, cozy, one-bedroom kind. The kitchen looks brand new and much to Raina's delight includes some automatic coffee machine with little cups for easy brewing. The French doors open onto a deck overlooking the churning Atlantic Ocean. Even with the cool, winter winds blowing off the ocean, we will definitely stay warm with either my naked body covering hers or, when we're not naked - which won't be often - the gas fireplace that's lit in the living area. It's a romantic setting, for sure.

We put our bags in the bedroom, where we find a large king-sized canopy bed decked out in all white in the middle of the room. Plenty of space for the 'or something' we love to do. I chuckle to myself at the memory. There's a large, flat-screen television hanging on the wall, but there are so many more exciting things to do in that room than watch TV. That sucker is staying off. Hide the fucking remote.

I turn to see Raina is gone, so I step toward the living room. I find her standing by the French doors, arms folded, head tucked down.

"Hey. You left me with that big bed all alone," I say, trying to lighten the mood somewhat.

Her body turns slightly. "Just thinking. I remember the time when Mom and Dad took me to Hatteras Island one year. There wasn't much to do, but Dad would spend the days building sandcastles with me. We would fill buckets and smooth out the sand to make the perfect palace." She gently pulls the window sheer aside and looks wistfully toward the ocean. "He'd take me out in the ocean on our boards, and we'd ride wave after wave until we had barely enough energy to make it back to our blanket. I didn't think much about it at the time, the memories we were making. I guess when all you have left are memories, they become a lifeline of sorts."

"I wish I would have been able to meet them. I didn't really have parents like that. It's not the same, but in some ways, I know what it feels like to no longer have a mother."

She turns to me, eyes wide. "Oh, God. I'm so sorry. That was insensitive. I got caught up in my own head and didn't even think about you.

"Sweetheart, I've come to terms with how I was raised. It wasn't anywhere near the life you had as a child, but I had my brother and we made our way just fine. I'm glad you never had to experience the kind of childhood I did. But I don't ever want you to feel sorry for me, got it? We were so young when Mom left us. I couldn't even begin to tell you the reasons why she did. I remember a few things about her, though. I remember her sitting Zander and me on her lap to read to us at night. And, unfortunately, I remember her cries when Dad would come home late from the bar. I didn't know it then, but now I know he was drunk. A lot."

There is no pity in her eyes and I'm glad. I don't need pity. The kindness in her eyes tells me she understands.

"Do you think you'll ever find your way back to your dad and your brother?"

My back stiffens, and I give it my best to not let her see how that question affects me. I look out at the ocean briefly, then turn back to her.

My hand runs through her hair and I pull her close to me. "No, that won't happen. What will happen though is you and me. We're building something here, angel. It's new and fresh and I don't know exactly where it will lead. I know where I hope it leads. But my dad has no place in our happiness."

"What about your brother? You were close once. You can mend broken fences, you know."

"What happened with my brother isn't something you can mend." Seconds. Seconds that feel like hours pass. And I say it. "Raina, my brother is dead."

I hear the gasp before I see the mortified expression on her face. Whatever the fuck prompted me to spit that out I'll never know, but it's out there now and I can't take it back.

"Oh my God, Zane. Why didn't you tell me? What happened?"

The memories are overpowering. They're coming back full force and I want to just run because I see him. I see him laying there. He's not breathing. Empty pill bottles and liquor bottles strewn on the floor. I can feel the walls closing in on me again.

Jesus, make it stop.

I force myself to shake off the bad memories before they overcome me. Instead, I look back up to the heavens for something, anything. I'm an idiot for telling her about this part of my life. But telling her seems like a little weight has been lifted off my shoulders. And isn't that just all sorts of fucked up. Feeling like this is confusing the hell out of me. "It's all in the past, Rain. I've dealt with it as best I could and moved on. That's why I moved away. Let's just talk about something else."

"When did it happen? Was it an accident?"

"Raina, stop!" She blinks a few times and backs up a step. Shit. God, I've got to get a handle on this, and right the fuck now. "Shit. I'm sorry. I didn't mean to yell. It's just a story I'd rather not get into. Maybe we can leave it for another time, okay? I promise."

I take her hand in mine and try pulling her back to me, the guilt of yet another lie, weighing on me. I know that I don't have it in me to tell her *another time*. I'd rather take it to my own grave.

"I'm the one who's sorry Zane. I didn't mean to pry. I was just so surprised you hadn't mentioned it. When you're ready, I'm here. You know that, right?"

She wipes a stray tear from her face and shifts on her feet, stepping toward me, encircling me in a hug. Her arms feel so good around me, her head on my chest. My arms move to surround her, I gently kiss the top of her head, and I just hold on. I hold on and pray for this one thing to work out in my life. I hold tight, sending up another prayer that Raina and I will be okay. We have to be okay. Not being okay isn't an option.

We stay like that for several minutes.

Joined together.
Two damaged souls.
Two broken hearts.
Connected, and healing.
For now.

Chapter Nineteen

RAINA

We stand there together for what seems like hours, even though only minutes pass. His brother is dead. His distance and reclusive personality are certainly understandable. Anyone who has lost a loved one has felt that acute pain and suffering so deep, that surfacing and living again can seem impossible. And right now, Zane and I are both bobbing at the surface, doing what we can to keep our heads above water. All this time he was trying to be there for me, drowning in his own hurt to help me heal mine. Selfless.

But I'm coming to terms with the fact that healing is absolutely possible. Zane and I will heal. Together.

Zane pulls back, and I can see him trying to find his center, his calm. He leans in to kiss me and we come together with understanding. With his mouth on mine, his hands begin running up and down my arms, coming up to cover my breasts. Our movements become more frenzied and before I can change positions, Zane has my shirt up over my head and is beginning to remove my jeans before gently laying me on the floor in front of the fireplace. This is Zane trying to forget.

He sits up on his knees and pulls his shirt over his head the way men do, and I'm reminded once again, of how beautifully formed this man truly is. He reaches back and unhooks my white, lacy bra...the one that matches my panties that I purchased for this trip. The look in his eyes as he sees them tells me he most definitely approves.

We lay together in front of the fire, sans clothes, and lose ourselves in each other for hours.

FEELING WARM AND SATED, and well into the night, we get up and make our way to the bedroom. On the way, I can hear his stomach rumble and laugh at the sound.

"In case you're wondering, the fridge and pantry are stocked. Let me see what I can round up for us."

"Why did the owners stock the fridge and pantry?"

"Because, angel, I called the agent and told him that I had a woman I would be ravishing here for days on end and would, in no uncertain terms, not be leaving this house. So, he agreed to stock the place, after a few laughs and a little encouragement from me."

"Zane, please tell me you didn't."

"Look in the fridge and you'll get your answer. And I am dead serious. I don't plan on letting you leave this house. I think I'll call you my prisoner." His eyebrows wiggle up and down in playfulness.

"Will you need to handcuff your prisoner?"

Zane takes my hands and grips them firmly behind my back. With his tongue, he licks along my neck, making me ache in all the right places. His voice comes out low and seductive in my ear. "If she attempts to escape, I'll be forced to. I'd hate to resort to such drastic measures, but for the safety of everyone around us, it may be necessary."

He can't see me, but I roll my eyes and smile. "Zane?"

"Yeah, baby?"

"Fix the food."

Zane throws back his head and laughs. "On it, angel."

§⃟

THE LIGHTS outside the house illuminate the beach and we have a perfect view of the ocean waves smashing against the shoreline. The sound provides a sense of contentment and calm. A sense of peace. The full moon shines down creating a magnificent reflection on the water, as stars light up the night sky. This getaway is just what I needed.

After we finish up our late dinner, we snuggle on the couch and turn on the TV to catch a movie. Not long after the movie begins, I hear a slight snore from Zane. He is sound asleep. After driving the distance to get here, and the emotional confession about his brother, I'm sure he could use some rest. I move out from under him to find my purse and text Sarah.

RAINA: **Hey girl. Here at the beach. All is well.**
SARAH: **Good to hear. Relax and enjoy that hunk of man! I'll just be here alone, living vicariously through you.**
R: **Lol! You need to find Liam and live it up yourself.**
S: **Eh. Maybe. Now get off the phone and get on that man. Naked!**
R: **Talk later! Love ya!!**
S: **Love ya chick! See you soon.**

I make my way back over to the sofa and snuggle back up

with Zane. Pulling a cover from the back of the sofa across us both, I sigh happily and close my eyes.

Before I could get comfortable again, Zane gets up, lifting me as if I weigh nothing, and carries me, bridal-style, back to the bedroom.

"Sleep, baby. Big day tomorrow." He leans in, kissing me on the top of my head.

"Night," I say yawning.

We snuggle in, and soon the thoughts running through my head quiet, and I fall into a deep sleep.

Chapter Twenty

ZANE

I open my eyes and see the sun shining brightly, filtering through the sheer curtains on the windows, although that shine can't hold a candle to Raina's smile. She lights up a room like a spotlight turned on at midnight. I lay with her a while, chuckling at how she's wrapped around me like a ribbon. Arms and legs tangled, hair fanned across the snow-white pillowcase, smooth and flawless, silky skin. Fucking perfect. And fucking mine.

I'm thankful that it's shaping up to be a sunny day today. It's perfect for walking along the beach and building a sand castle with Raina. She remembers doing those things with her family, so I'm hoping those are memories I can make with her, too. She'll be in for a surprise when we get back from our beach time, and I'm anxious just thinking about it. It took a bit of coercing to set this up, but she's worth every headache I went through to do it.

She's still sound asleep, which is not surprising, considering how many times I woke her up last night with my mouth, only to bury myself so deep inside her, I thought I may never come out. Making love to her has to be the most unforgettable experience of my life. Sex is so different with her.

Extraordinary.

Passionate.

Consuming.

Everything I've ever wanted is laying right alongside me, our hearts beating in sync with one another like two drums tapping out a rhythm. I can't help but think we were brought together under the most screwed-up circumstances for a reason. She's like my lifeline now. My salvation.

"Hey, baby?" Her eyes remain closed. "Angel?" She's sleeping like the dead and as much as I don't want to wake her, I want to get our day started. I'm excited about the holidays for the first time in a long time. And I can't wait to share it with Raina.

"You gonna wake up anytime soon? It's a beautiful day outside." Nothing. "Almost as beautiful as your sweet tasting and sweet smelling..."

"Zane," she interrupts, eyes still closed. That little shit has been awake this whole time. "Honey, can you not finish that thought?" she says, nearly laughing. "I can't keep up with you. You're like that bunny that keeps going and going."

"Noted. Now get up. We've got shit to do." I smack her on the ass as I let out a hearty laugh at her comparison and hop out of bed, throwing on my sweats. She is right, though. I do have stamina, and a vigorous sex drive, but I haven't heard her complain till now. Although, I think that's more of an 'I'm-not-a-morning-person' whine than anything.

"What shit do we have to do? We're on vacation!" she whines again, pulling the covers back up over her sweet body.

"We've got a sand castle to build, darlin'. Buckets and shovels are in the closet by the door." Next to her screams of ecstasy last night, the ones where I think our neighbors were introduced to my name, her squeals and her smile at the thought of building sand castles like she did when she was a little girl, is just about the finest sound I could ever hope to hear. She's genuinely happy. And I did that for her.

She scrambles out of bed to get dressed. I love her enthusiasm.

Love.

Breakfast is rushed so we can get to the beach. We bundle up, braving the cool winds, and build ourselves a one-of-a-kind sandcastle. In reality, it looks nothing like a castle, but we're having a blast, and it is so good to see Raina enjoying her day. She talks about how her dad would become so serious about building sandcastles, and how he would use plastic knives and other tools to carve the details just right. The castle was formed with military precision. I think our little castle suffers by comparison because neither one of us gets that into it, but she seems surprisingly happy to share that memory, and I'm all too happy to listen.

We pile the sand buckets and shovels together by the steps leading up to the house, and take off down the beach for a walk, hand in hand. The sun is quickly becoming concealed by the ominous, gray clouds, the ocean breeze is blowing Raina's beautiful hair all around, and it feels like perhaps rain is on the way. We turn around after a mile or so to head back to the house. Along the way, Raina bends to gather a few seashells before they become submerged in the wet sand after the waves retreat back into the sea.

"These are beautiful. I have a bowl of shells at my apartment from when dad and I collected them years and years ago. I can add these to my collection."

I put my arm around her shoulder and pull her close to me, giving her that show of silent support she needs while she recalls her memories. Leaning over, I kiss her on top of her head.

"I'd love to see that collection sometime. I don't remember seeing it when I was at your place before."

Raina looks up to me, with peace in her eyes. "I've never gotten it out of the box. Think maybe it's time?"

"I think that would be great. Those times with your folks were priceless, and now they're memories. I think they would love knowing you're remembering the good times with them. Remembering is a way of holding on to them and keeping them close even though they're gone."

"You are a wise man, Zane. You make me feel so much better."

She looks at me and hesitates for a moment. "If you ever want to talk about your brother and the memories you have of him, I'd love to hear them."

"Someday, angel. Someday."

I fight against myself to not turn away from her, to stay strong. She needs stability and comfort and understanding, even love. I can give her all those things, but I have to forget my own feelings of anger. Anger at my dad for the bullshit he put Zander and me through growing up, and even anger at my brother, for leaving me and taking the easy way out.

Right at this moment, my resolve strengthens, and I vow to be everything Raina needs. I just hope in doing that, I can overcome my own demons. Move on. And love Raina as much as she deserves.

"Zane, I can actually feel you thinking right now. Can I help?"

"You help more than you know," I say, as we continue strolling through the sand. "Just being here with me, sharing your stories and your life with me, makes everything better. Believe me, it helps."

I can feel the guilt stirring up inside of me again, so I stop and turn her face to me, taking it in my hands. Pulling her close, I kiss her, allowing my love for her to bleed right through to her heart. When I kiss her like this, I forget. I forget what I'm keeping from her, and I also forget the past.

"Let's get back up to the house. There's a surprise there for you...I hope."

"I love surprises! Race ya," she challenges.

"Oh, baby. It's on."

We take off running through the cold sand, up to the weathered, wooden steps and toward the house. Before I can reach her to grab her around the waist, she stops dead in her tracks when she sees the Christmas tree through the large window that faces the ocean. Both hands come to her mouth as she turns to look at me with watery eyes.

"Baby, what's wrong?"

"Nothing. Not one thing. Zane, you have just given me the best Christmas present I've had since Mom and Dad died." Her hands move to cover her entire, beautiful face, but I pull them away and replace them with my own resting on her cheeks.

"Babe?"

"I never thought I'd want to celebrate Christmas again. I can't believe you did this for me. I haven't put up a tree since..." she whispers, trying to fight the tears.

"This surprise is only the tip of the iceberg. I want to spend the rest of my life making you happy."

"The rest of your life?" she nervously asks.

"Raina, I love you, baby. When I look at you I see a future I never thought I'd have. I know we haven't been together that long, but when the heart knows, it knows. You're it for me."

She buries her face in my chest and weeps. Not quite the reaction I was hoping for, but I know, without a doubt, those tears are not ones of sadness. After taking a moment to pull herself together, she peers up at me, smiling beautifully with a stray tear tumbling down her cheek. If it's possible, I just fell more in love with her at this very moment.

"Truthfully, I wasn't sure I'd ever be this happy again. But then I met you and the happiness I thought I'd lost, I found. Because of you. I love you too, Zane. With all my heart."

As a faint roll of thunder resonates from the heavens, I take Raina's hand and walk with her to the beach house. We stand in the doorway, and it almost feels like a renewal of some kind. Like when we walk through that door, we'll begin a new life together. It's what I optimistically long for. A lifetime with my angel.

Chapter Twenty-One

RAINA

I'm not at all certain what it is about this man that confuses me most. The broodiness that changes almost instantly into the happiness I see now, or the way he continually catches me by surprise at every turn. When I first laid eyes on that Christmas tree, I felt the Earth move under my feet. It was an unexpected surprise, to say the least. As we stood in the doorway to the beach house, I began to imagine, for the first time, what my life would be like with Zane. I could envision the home we would build together, children - a whole pack of them - and a lifetime of happiness. I imagined holidays and vacations and taking long walks and planning our future. So many things that I really never dreamed of again after my parents died.

This man has resuscitated those dreams in my mind. He's helped me see that I deserve that happiness and helped me realize I do have a wonderful future ahead of me. And I want it to be with him.

I know Zane would love to do more with his life than tend bar, and I want to be the one to encourage him to follow his dreams, whatever they may be. He's endured a great loss in his life, just as I have. And he deserves to be loved.

We're just two people who were left all alone, so alike in many ways, and now we're creating a relationship that was conceived from hurt and pain but will surely blossom into something remarkable.

We enter the house and I walk toward the sparkling, lighted Christmas tree. It's like a thousand night stars twinkling in the sky. It's magical, enchanting. And the kindest thing anyone has ever done for me. My steps are slow, but no longer reluctant. Gazing at the lights, I feel Zane come up behind me, enveloping me in his arms, his lips on my neck, stranded there for minutes, breathing me in.

"I had the realtor guy who stocked the house get a tree too. I think I owe him a kidney at this point."

I can't help but smile, thinking of all the trouble he went through to make this trip so special for me. "I'm certain you do. I could never have imagined a holiday like this, with you. Thank you."

"Merry Christmas, angel."

I laugh a little, then turn in his arms, my ear snuggled close to his chest, listening to the rhythm of a beating heart. His heart. At one time in my life, I thought I may no longer have the capacity to love deeply again. I was uncertain as to whether Zane did either, when I first met him. I know that to be untrue now. I love this man. This tall, dark, handsome, and compassionate man.

"Rain? Did you hear me?"

"I did. I was just thinking," I say, looking up and smiling, resting my hand on his cheek. "Merry Christmas to you too."

He pulls out a beautiful sprig of mistletoe from his back pocket, with bright green leaves and deep red berries, and dangles it over my head. My head shakes with laughter. "I'm not even going to ask. I hope you'll do well with just one kidney."

"He was more than happy to help. He's an older man. Said he used to do the same kinds of things for his wife. Said that's what kept their marriage new and fresh...that he always kept her on her toes and made her smile with surprises."

"He sounds like a wonderful man with a very lucky wife. So what do you plan to do now that I'm under the mistletoe?"

Zane smacks his hand against his heart. "You wound me. Do you even have to ask that question? For starters, I'm going to drag you into my cave, thump my chest, and make you my woman."

"I don't think that's how mistletoe works."

"Oh, sweetheart, just watch. My mistletoe is magic. You'll be entranced, mystified."

I laughing out loud as I'm hoisted up over Zane's shoulder. He hauls me into the bedroom, drops me awkwardly in the middle of the king-sized bed, and he proceeds to take complete control of my pleasure.

My clothes are removed and heaped into a pile on the floor, along with his. His movements are hurried, as if he can't get inside me quick enough. My breath comes out in short gasps, my pulse pounding erratically, as his tongue glosses over my neck where he bites down gently. His hands circle my breasts, then glide down my stomach and pause at the juncture of my thighs, teasing there, causing my back to arch off the bed. He gently pushes me back down and holds me there, covering me, controlling me with his body. I can feel the wetness already, and he knows I'm ready for him.

"You are a vision. Breathtaking."

"Please..." I beg.

"You need me, baby? Need me inside of you? Put your arms on the headboard. Leave them there. Understand?"

I don't even get the word out before he slams into me, filling me, consuming me. The sting is secondary to the pleasure he brings. He begins moving at a frantic pace and my hips flex upward to keep in time with his rhythm. Our bodies fuse as one. He raises slightly, pulling my legs over his shoulders, as he moves inside me, and the look in his eyes sets my soul on fire. Passion and love. More than I could ever imagine, but everything I'd hoped for.

"I completely lose myself with you, Raina."

"Then lose yourself with me. And I'll find you. I'll find you every time."

The onslaught of Zane's passion continues at a frenzied pace and spurs my orgasm to life. "Let go, baby. Come." And I do. I come like never before and Zane soon follows.

We lay together on the bed in each other's arms. Sated, complete. Zane is swirling his fingers in my hair, and the sensation begins to lull me to sleep.

I feel the covers sliding up over my body, warming the places that aren't touching Zane. His body is like a furnace, keeping me warm and toasty on these long, cool, winter nights. My heavy eyelids fight hard to stay open, but soon give up the battle and close peacefully.

I AWAKEN to the sound of raindrops pelting against the windows of the house, surrounded in darkness. My sense of smell kicks into high gear, as the aroma of bacon drifts into the bedroom. The contrasting scent of cinnamon and bread linger in the air, mixing with salty bacon.

Why breakfast at 5:00 in the morning?

I stumble out of bed and grab Zane's tee to throw on, then head toward the kitchen. I think me in his tee is his favorite. As I'm walking, I pull my hair up into a messy bun to keep it out of my eyes. It's still dark outside, but inside, the Christmas tree lights glisten like thousands of tiny, shimmering diamonds. The sweet, woodsy smell of fresh pine hits my nose, mixing with the aroma of breakfast foods wafting from the kitchen. I turn from the beautiful sight of the tree, then stop and take in the sight before me. Zane, shirtless, with low-hanging sweats covering his backside.

Well, Merry Christmas to me. I think those sweatpants are my favorite gift ever.

I can sense Zane turning around, but my eyes stay glued to that glorious body that I am oh so lucky to sleep next to every night.

"Angel? Hey. Eyes up here, babe." He laughs as he makes a V with his fingers and pointing them towards his face.

Yep, busted.

"Hey," I sigh. "What are you doing up so early?"

"It's Christmas, babe. You hungry?"

I shake the sleepiness out of my head. "Very." He reaches into the oven to pull out the cinnamon rolls as he turns down the heat on the sizzling bacon. Eggs are sitting on the counter, up next in the skillet, apparently.

"Have a seat. I set up your coffee. Just press the button. Juice too?" he asks, as he continues to prepare this culinary delight.

"Give me the works."

Zane finishes preparing our breakfast and we sit comfortably together. It's delicious, and I wonder how he learned to cook. He mentioned his dad never really bothered with him or his brother. They most likely had to fend for themselves, which makes me sad to think about Christmas for those two growing up. I consider how fortunate I was to have my parents for as long as I did, knowing Zane really had no one at all. Just his brother. And now his brother is gone too. I shake those depressing thoughts from my mind, thankful that he and I are enjoying this holiday together, and I smile, knowing that I'm making him happy.

We clean up the kitchen together and make small talk as we do.

"Let me get you another cup of coffee. Go sit on the sofa."

As soon as I'm comfortable, Zane walks in with my drink in one hand, and in the other is a small gift-wrapped box.

"Merry Christmas, baby."

"That poor agent you've sent running all over Wrightsville. He's going to be happy to see us leave."

Zane laughs out loud. "No, angel. I bought this back home and brought it with me. Now open it, smart ass."

I anxiously unwrap the package and when I open the lid to the jewelry box, tears being to fill my eyes. It's obvious that Zane remembers the seemingly trivial things because inside the box is a beautiful butterfly necklace. Butterflies. Like the ones on the frame at my apartment. The frame that holds the picture of Mom and Dad.

"Zane, it's beautiful. How did you...?"

My heart swells, and I have to stop to catch my breath before the tears spill over. I lift the necklace out of the box and hand it to him to put around my neck. He fastens the latch, caressing the back of my neck with his soft lips. His hand run firmly down my arms and stop at my hands, like a protector. He whispers into my ear.

"I saw that in one of the little shops in town. I thought of you and that frame where you keep your parents' picture. Figured you'd maybe like it." He speaks hesitantly, not quite sure of himself.

"It's stunning. It's perfect." I spin around to show him. "How does it look?"

Zane hesitates for just a second. "Stunning. And perfect." He smiles, quite proud of himself. "It'll look even better without that t-shirt on. Maybe just the necklace? Try that and let me see how it looks that way."

I roll my eyes at the way Zane goes from serious to playful, like he's not quite sure how to take the compliments I'm giving him. It's likely that growing up he never had much of a chance to give or receive presents at any time of year, so I remind myself to let him know throughout the day how perfect and thoughtful the necklace really is.

"How about *not* right now. Stay right there. I've got to get something out of my bag." I jaunt into the bedroom, and pull out my bag, unzipping the hidden pocket and retrieve the gift I got for Zane.

When I return to the sofa, he's sitting there drinking my coffee and nearly spills it when he sees me. He has become a closet coffee lover I just know it. I raise my eyebrows and shoot him an ornery grin.

"Merry Christmas," I say, as I bounce down on the sofa beside him and I hand him his gift.

Before he even opens it, he leans over, reaches his hand around the back of my neck and pulls me close to him, whispering, "Tell me there's lingerie in this teeny tiny box. You know, the black kind. Or maybe a sexy little white lace number like the bra and panties you've worn before."

It takes me a minute to recover from the deep, sexy tone of his voice whispering in my ear. I swallow hard and try not to smile. "You're hilarious. Now, no. Just open it. Before you get me all...you know."

"Oh, I know, babe. I most assuredly know. And for the record, I take the subject of your lingerie very seriously," he says, winking at me.

Zane opens the package quickly to find a personalized coffee mug, and he laughs the most heartfelt, genuine laugh I've ever heard from him.

"Now *that* is perfect. You are the master gift giver, angel. I love it."

"Look down inside the cup. There's more."

Zane roots through the tissue paper and unwraps the next gift.

"A key?"

"To my place. You know, so if you want to be there when I get home from school, you can. Or not. Or whatever. I mean if you don't want that, it's okay. I really just..."

"Babe. Stop. Are you sure?"

"I've never been more sure. I want you to have it. I even cleaned out a drawer in the bathroom for some of your, you know, bathroom stuff."

Zane's smile gets bigger and bigger. He is loving every single minute of my stammering and making a fool of myself. I feel the heat rush to my cheeks at the same time he grabs me and pulls me over to him so I'm straddling his lap.

"These three gifts are by far the best I've ever received."

I look at him questioningly.

He uses his fingers to tick them off. "The mug, the key, and you. Best. Christmas. Ever," he says accentuating each word with a kiss.

We fall into a warm embrace, comfortable and secure. These special moments with Zane are the most endearing. It's so perfect that I wonder if it will always be this amazing with him.

Chapter Twenty-Two

ZANE

Spending Christmas with Raina is everything I thought it would be. We're making our way back to Hillsborough and the thought of coming out of the little beachfront cocoon that was ours the past few days causes disappointment. It was as if there, nothing could touch us. No one knew us and we could relax. Along the route home, we pass a few signs for Raleigh and my insides churn at the thought of my father still being there, somewhere, and the fact that he knows about the accident.

I quickly banish that thought from my mind, not wanting to ruin the last bit of time left before we make it home. I shake off those intrusive thoughts and make conversation with Raina about starting back to school in January. It's a welcome distraction.

Shortly after we arrive at the apartment, Raina gets a call from Sarah to welcome her home. She takes her cell in the bedroom and talks while she unpacks dirty clothes, not that there were many. I make myself at home on her sofa and kick back, closing my eyes to relive the memories of our time together. When she comes to sit by me after the call, her face is etched with confusion and concern.

"Zane, the bar opened back up last night, and Sarah was there with Liam. She said some man came in looking for you. Said he didn't know where you lived and wanted to check around to find out. He never said who he was, but could it be your dad?"

Fuck. Fuck, fuck, fuck. This can't be happening. What the hell does he want?

I can feel my muscles tense throughout my body, and I can only hope Raina doesn't take notice.

"I guess it could be. Did she say what he looked like?"

Raina describes the man and sure enough, he sounds just like dear old Dad. Apparently, he came in last evening - thank God I wasn't there - asking if anyone knew me or where I lived. Thankfully, Sam didn't tell him anything. Unfortunately, he knows I'm in Hillsborough and this isn't a big enough place to hide from someone who wants to find you. He's such a piece of shit. Doesn't take much to convince me he'll hang around till he finds me.

"Rain, I want you to stay away from him if he ever comes around the bar when you're there. He's poison and I don't want you around that shit."

"Okay, but you know I can help you. I can be there to support you, whatever you need."

"*No,*" I say too quickly. "I mean, no. Please tell me you'll stay away from him."

"Okay. If that's what you want. You just seem so tense now. I say just find out what he wants and send him on his way," she says timidly.

This is not good. Not good at all. What the fuck do I do now? I get up from the sofa and begin pacing back and forth. I'm suddenly agitated as fuck and I can't sit still. I run my hands through my hair, stopping at my neck. I stretch it in an attempt to relieve some tension.

"Just keep your distance. It's better if he doesn't interact with you at all. I don't want him to look at you, or even know about you. Maybe he'll head back to Raleigh if he can't find me anywhere. Promise me you'll stay away."

"I promise. I'll steer clear." She looks at me, confused. I begin to feel the weight of guilt weighing on me again. Jesus, can't anything be simple and just go my way for a change?

I sigh and close my eyes, praying that whatever he wants isn't going to cause me any problems. I'm not very optimistic, though. Nothing to do with him is ever straightforward. There is something he wants. I just have to find out what it is and keep him away from Rain.

Chapter Twenty-Three

RAINA

I spend much of the rest of my holiday vacation with Zane, most of it at my place. I could sense how agitated he was and it was cause for concern. There is something between him and his dad, more than just his dad being a shit parent. It's difficult to imagine what life was like for him as a child. Taking that into account, I decide that Zane just wants nothing to do with that man, and who could blame him.

Sarah and I go to the pub Friday night. She wants to see Liam again, which is totally a good thing. In the past, she hadn't had a relationship last longer than a week, but she seems completely smitten with Liam and I couldn't be happier for her. Liam is a good guy. Funny how she tells me they're just friends.

Sarah and I sit at a table near the front to listen to the music. Tira is waitressing tonight and is content to spend more time glaring at me than waiting on customers, but whatever. I have neither the time nor inclination to concern myself with her any longer.

I look up to find Zane at the bar, just in time to see him

turn and walk back toward the office, phone in hand. I walk to the bar to get a few more drinks and talk to Sam, hoping he can fill me in on how Zane has been acting at work, but get nothing more than normal. Tira brushes past me, nearly causing me to spill the drinks on my way back to the table. Jealousy doesn't look good on her. She's beautiful and can have any man she wants, but for whatever reason, she wants Zane. I turn to watch her move toward the office as well, stopping at the partially-opened door. She stands there, clearly listening to his conversation. *What is she up to?*

Shaking my head, I walk back to the table. The guys are on a set break and Liam has made his way to the seat beside Sarah. Deciding to give those two an opportunity to talk, I hand Sarah her drink, then return to the bar, to find my usual seat and wait for Zane to return from the office. Tira parades past me again, this time sneering at me.

"Oh, this is good. Too, too good, dear Raina," she announces as she passes by.

Abruptly I stand and grab her by the arm to spin her toward me. "What the hell is your problem, Tira?"

"Oh, I don't have a problem. But you will. Why don't you ask Zane about the little conversation he was having with his dad? I'm sure you'll find it...enlightening." She smirks and turns around, strolling toward the tables. I can hear her laughing, and the anger rises up in me almost instantly.

I decide to sit back down at my barstool and wait for Zane to come out of the office. When he does, he sees me at the bar and stops in his tracks. He remains rooted to his spot right outside the office door, like a statue, and the look on his face is haunting. There is a storm raging in my man's eyes, a shadowy darkness surrounding him. This is not good. Whatever that conversation was about has him completely unhinged. And Tira knows.

I can't help but think to myself that years ago, my life was simple. I lived in a simple home, with two wonderful parents, celebrating holidays, taking family vacations. I was working in a mall and getting a teaching degree. Right at this moment, my life is nearly unrecognizable and nowhere near simple. No home, just an apartment on my own, in a completely different town, and no parents to look to for guidance. Add in one complex bartender and one jealous bitch, and I'd say that's a recipe for a disaster that I'd rather avoid. Yet here I am, in the middle of some fiasco I didn't really ask to be a part of.

He slowly makes his way to the bar and stops in front of me, wave after wave of tension rolling off his body.

"Zane, what's wrong? What's happened?"

He pulls in his breath as if it's his last one. His eyes look vacant and as he exhales, he drops his head. After a moment, he looks at me and I see turmoil and guilt overtake him.

"You're scaring me. What's wrong?"

"My dad knows I'm here, that I work here. Apparently, he ran into Tira as he was walking out the door when he left here looking for me the other day. She told him she knew me and to call me here at the bar. That's how he found out."

"Well, you knew he was looking for you. You seem so surprised."

Silence.

"We have to talk."

There has never been a time in my life when those words have ever amounted to anything but pain and suffering. I am completely frozen. I don't know where to look, what to say. So I continue to stare blankly into Zane's eyes, hoping against hope that I'm wrong. Memories begin to assault my mind. My ex telling me he was leaving me. My parent's death. Agony. Loneliness. Anguish.

It's then that Sam makes his way toward us, and it's clear

something is very wrong. He tells Zane he's called his wife to come in to help him finish out the evening, and that he can take the remainder of the night off.

"Let's go." His face, expressionless.

I follow closely behind him and look over at Sarah. She looks concerned, and I hold up my thumb and pinky like a phone to my ear and mouth the words, *I'll call you later*. She sends a sad smile my way, but I have nothing to give her in return.

Tira makes her way over to us as we try to leave the pub. "That was some conversation you had with your dad there." Zane is furious and spins around to face her.

"What the hell? You were listening?" Zane is ready to strike. He points his finger directly at her. "You say nothing. You say abso-fucking-lutely nothing. Got me?"

"Oh, Zane. Your secret's safe with me," she coos, her hand running up and down his arm. "Although I don't think your Raina here is going to like it one little bit," her tone changing as she nods her head my way.

Zane turns back around and pulls me with him toward the door. We exit the building and walk briskly to his car. I stop him mid-stride, hoping he'll calm down. On his face, there hopelessness I see as he turns around to me. His eyes are empty. The love that had taken over where the hurt used to be is no longer visible. It's been replaced with guilt and desperation, and it feels as though he'd rather be anywhere but here with me.

I can feel tears building in my eyes, but a deep breath calms me enough to speak. "Zane, tell me what's going on. What's Tira talking about?"

"We'll talk at home. I can't do this here," he says, as we continue walking to the car.

"Let's go to my apartment." My feelings are spinning out

of control. Whatever this is, it can't be good. So at least when he delivers whatever blow is coming - the one that will no doubt crush me - I'll be at home, safe. Relatively anyway.

Zane opens the car door for me, and I get in. He waits there for a moment, looking upward to the sky, inhaling deeply, then shuts my door. Once in the driver's seat, he starts the engine and with both hands on the steering wheel, looks at me. I fidget with the hem of my shirt, trying to keep myself calm, not wanting to look at the tension I know I'll see on Zane's face. I can almost feel the weight on my shoulders getting heavier and heavier, like I'm being pulled by the strong waves of the ocean. There was a time when the sound of the waves soothed my soul. Now they threaten to drag me under.

ONCE WE'RE in my apartment, Zane sits on my sofa, offering his hand in an attempt to bring me closer to him. I'm so keyed up at this point, I don't think I'm capable of sitting, but I make my way to the sofa, trying to settle, and sit down beside him, knowing I won't be there for long.

"There are things in my past that you need to know about. There's a reason why I didn't tell you before and I hope, God I hope and pray you understand. Please let me tell you everything; you need to hear the whole story." He turns to face me, looking remorseful. I don't like that look.

"Go on," I say, trying to find my resolve.

"I've told you before that my dad was a terrible father. A drunk. He was hardly ever around, but when he was, he would scream at Zander and me constantly. We practically raised ourselves. We had a neighbor that would look out for us. She would give us hand-me-down clothes that belonged to her two older sons. A lot of nights, we would come home from school to an empty fridge, so we'd walk to her house and she would always have something for us to eat."

He hesitates. "Zander and I were twins."

Zane looks up as I gasp. Zander is dead. Zane lost his twin.

His breath hitches slightly, but he continues, struggling with sharing his past.

"Zander was most definitely the more outgoing of the two of us. He was so high spirited and energetic. He was so friendly to everyone, and he was always the life of the party. Didn't always make good decisions either," he says, shaking his head, "which meant I was left cleaning up a lot of his messes. I didn't mind, though. I knew he was trying to make up for the shitty childhood we had. Trying to make everyone believe we had a perfect life.

"He started drinking after we got out of high school and he drank a lot. He couldn't hold a job because of it. I would go to parties, or the bar, or sometimes to some God-forsaken back alley to pick him up, so he didn't drive himself home. I ended up losing a job over that. Having to leave in the middle of the workday to get him wasn't bad until it was happening a few times a week. But I did what I had to do. And I wouldn't change that. He was all I had."

I watch Zane intently, and suddenly tears begin to fall from his eyes. He is completely wrecked and I've never felt such sadness coming from him. No longer talking, he wipes the tears away with his shirt sleeve. After a few minutes, he goes on.

"The drinking got really bad, and one morning he came home after a night of being completely drunk, barely able to stand. He had gone to pick up Dad, was talked into hanging there with him and his so-called friends, and started drinking. Eventually, they both got into the car. He dropped Dad off at his house, slept off his drunk in the car, and came back the next morning to the apartment we were sharing. Once he made it into the living room, he fell onto the sofa. He kept saying he was sorry and that...that he didn't mean it. Raina, he kept saying it was an accident, that he didn't even see them walking."

I freeze, my breath stolen from my lungs. Zane's words are like a razor-sharp arrow and my heart is the bright red center of the target. This can't be happening.

Oh, my God. It was Zane's brother. He killed them. A wave of nausea hits me like a tsunami and I hold my stomach, praying I don't vomit all over the floor.

With tears spilling over and down my cheeks I whisper, "Oh God, please Zane, tell me no. Tell me it wasn't him."

Zane moves closer and attempts to take my hand, but I pull it away. Instead of looking at me, he stares at the floor, shaking his head. It's what he doesn't say right at that moment that speaks the loudest. I know the answer without hearing a word.

I try to stand, only to fall from the couch to my knees, utterly destroyed. I'm reliving my parent's death all over again and I know this time, I will not survive. A scream comes from deep within my gut, and sharply penetrates the silence inside my apartment. Zane lowers himself beside me and tries to help me stand, but I shove him away, standing on my own.

"You knew? You knew it was your brother, and you didn't tell me?" My fists are primed, and I rush towards him taking shot after shot at his chest, screaming, "I hate you!" over and over again. "How could you do this to me?"

He stands there, rooted in his stance, allowing me to pummel his body with blow after blow. Allowing me to fall apart. My knees buckle again, and Zane is there to catch my fall.

"Please, baby. It's not like that, I need to explain," he says, holding my arms with his hands.

"Leave!" My screams splinter the air inside, causing Zane to step back.

"Rain..."

"No. You need to leave."

With my arms wrapped around myself, I keep my head down, my stomach churning, ready to expel everything I'd eaten that day. My head throbs and I am racked with pain like I've never known. My heart physically breaks...all over again.

Zane tries to reach out to me, but I scramble out of his way and meet his gaze. "Get out, Zane. Don't ever come back." My voice trembles, no longer sounding like my own.

"Please, Raina, please. Just listen. It's not..."

"You lied to me! Get out now! I won't say it again." I look at him one last time with disdain and outrage. And I see every horrible secret in the deepest part of him. Ones that are secrets no longer.

He steps slowly back toward the door.

I turn away from him and close my eyes, in an attempt to hide from the pain, the anger, the devastation. All I can hear are the sobs coming from inside my shattered soul.

No movement. No voices, but then a faint, quivering whisper. "I love you, Rain. I'll always love you, angel."

The door shuts quietly.

I collapse, nearly breathless, and sit huddled and motionless on the floor, sobbing, and paralyzed from the emotional hurt I've just endured.

I'm alone again.

I'm shattered.

Destroyed.

The pain is excruciating.

I weep and weep.

Eventually, there are no more tears left to cry. All that remains is the salty taste on my lips. In my heart, there is an emptiness, a hollowness that Zane used to fill.

Chapter Twenty-Four

RAINA

S till on the floor of my apartment, my eyes make a weak attempt to open when I hear a faint knock on the door. I have no desire to open my eyes because then I'll be forced to face the truth that was uncovered tonight.

The knock comes again, louder than before. "Raina?" The knocking continues.

It's Sarah.

I roll to my side and push myself to stand, holding onto the arm of the sofa for stability. Making my way over to the door, I stumble and grab onto the counter to right myself. I can't think. I can't feel.

It takes all my strength to pull open the door, and Sarah rushes in.

"What are you doing here?" I whisper and turn back around to head back to the living area. I need to sit.

"Zane called. Jesus, Raina, what the hell happened?"

"He called you? Didn't he tell you?"

"No. He just said I needed to get here and to not waste any time doing it. I was scared to death. What's going on?"

I curl up on the end of the sofa and lean against the arm, pulling my feet up and locking my arms around them. I turn my head to the side and rest it on my knees.

"Zane has a twin. Zander. He's dead. Thank God."

"Jesus, Raina, how can you say that? That's not like you at all. You don't even know him...do you?" she asks, seeming more and more confused. She takes a seat as I suck in a deep breath knowing I'll have to tell her.

"Technically, no. What I do know is that he was the drunk that hit my parents and killed them." I can barely get those painful words past my lips. "Zane knew. He was talking to his dad and Tira overheard. He had to tell me. Tira really left him no choice. Makes me wonder if he would have ever said anything to me, or if he just told me because of her."

"Oh my God. Are you sure?"

"Unquestionably sure. Zane told me about his brother. About the morning he came home after the accident. He didn't come right out and say it was his brother, but when I asked if Zander was the one who hit my parents, he went dead silent, which was very telling. He couldn't even admit it. He knew the whole time."

Taking a deep breath, I fight back more tears.

"Jesus. I just can't comprehend all this. So him being in Hillsborough was a coincidence? Some kind of fluke?"

I lift my head to meet Sarah's eyes. "I don't think it was. He had to have known about me. You know, I always wondered what he saw in me. I guess he really didn't see a thing. I was someone he just felt sorry for...a pity fuck. Poor little Raina, all alone."

Sarah sits up straighter and speaks firmly. "That's bullshit and you know it. I can't for the life of me imagine what the hell he was thinking, but the way he looks at you, the way he takes care of you and the things he does for you? That doesn't scream pity fuck to me. There has to be more to this.

You have to talk to him because I think you owe it to yourself to hear the whole story, no matter how painful that may be. Maybe not tonight or even next week, but soon, babe. And don't argue. You know I'm right."

"Right now, I need to sleep, Sarah. I can barely function, and my head is spinning. Is it okay if I call you tomorrow?"

"Do you need me to stay? I can stay," she says, reaching for me.

"No. I just need some time to think. Or maybe I don't even need to think at all. I don't know. Thanks for coming to check on me."

Sarah gets up and slowly makes her way to the door, and I follow quietly behind. She holds onto the doorknob and pauses briefly, turning to me. "You know Zane was still outside your door when I got here. He was sitting on the floor, leaning against it. I don't think I've ever seen someone look so pitiful. He just asked me to take care of you. Then he got up and left."

My mind can't process those words right now. I can't even begin to think about that, because then it'll make me feel sorry for him. Right now, all I want to feel is pure hatred.

"He doesn't get to...never mind. He's gone. Good night, Sarah."

She pulls me in for another long hug, holding on and taking care of me.

"Night, babe. Call me tomorrow, okay?"

"Sure," I mumble.

I watch Sarah leave, and for the second time tonight, the door closes gingerly. And for the second time tonight, I'm alone in the silence. A powerful scream inside my head. A deafening cry.

God help me.

I drag myself into the bedroom, and curl up in my comforter, but find no comfort in it at all. Time heals all wounds? That's bullshit. Nothing will ever heal these wounds. I have been painfully, heinously, ripped open again, my soul left battered and beaten. The butterfly necklace Zane gave me rests on my nightstand. It's funny that when I first met Zane, it was like feeling a million butterflies in my stomach, fluttering nervously around. And really, butterflies *are* beautiful, but their lives are fleeting. Ironically, the man I thought I could live the rest of my life with is the one who, for all intents and purposes, ended it tonight. A pity, really. I finally felt as though I was just starting to live again. But, the proverbial rug has been pulled out from under me one more time. And I wonder when I'll ever learn.

So, my heart will lock itself away, and I'll begin to go through the motions of life. That's how I managed in the past and that's how it will be now. And I'll be okay. Mostly.

Chapter Twenty-Five

ZANE

I have destroyed the only good, pure, and perfect thing that has ever come into my life. Obliterated it. Smashed beyond recognition. The look on Raina's face as she yelled for me to get out of her apartment was one of complete devastation. I put that there. It's all my fault.

What kind of heartless idiot am I? I fucking *knew* this wouldn't end well. I knew it, but I did it anyway.

My angel.

I sat outside her apartment with my back against her door, until I finally reached Sarah on her cell. Listening to the sobs and cries of my angel nearly broke me in two. She has such a capacity to love, to care, and it's hard not to be completely captivated by her. I can't help but feel I have destroyed that. I deserve this pain, this torment. Every single fucking bit of it.

In my apartment, I continue to sit in the uncomfortable chair by the window, staring blankly, watching a few stray snowflakes make their way to the ground. The air outside is cold, but my heart feels even colder.

I wanted to explain the entire situation to Raina. She

needed to hear it. I was at a complete loss last night trying to explain this fucking mess, and I fucked everything up. But then again, how the hell did I think this would play out. I tricked myself into believing Raina would never find out. Joke's on me, apparently. But Jesus, I had no idea the depths of my father's depravity. He will burn in hell one day for what he's done. His actions are reprehensible.

I grab a few clothes, my wallet, and keys and head out into the cold and gloomy early morning air. I get in my car and head straight to Raleigh. My father will not get away with this. He sure as hell blindsided me during that phone call, but I clearly see now what I have to do.

THE DRIVE to Raleigh goes by more quickly than I realize and soon enough, I'm pulling into the shithole I lived in for years with Zander and Dad. His beat up car is parked haphazardly in the driveway. Drove home drunk again, most likely. Seems to be his MO. The lights are on, but that doesn't mean anything. He's too fucking lazy to turn them off when he leaves. Of course, the only place he ever seems to go is the bar. As I walk around the back side of the house, the stench of garbage nauseates me and I see the trash bags piled up near the cellar door. The cement steps leading up into the kitchen are littered with fallen leaves and empty beer cans, and the screen door is hanging lopsided. Disgusting. It's hard to imagine how Zander and I ever lived in a dump like this.

I walk into the house and find Dad passed out on the couch, the TV blaring, and empty beer cans scattered on the floor. He's a mess. Dirty clothes, and hair that looks as though it hasn't been washed in weeks. A real gem.

I kick his legs to wake him up. "Get up you piece of shit!"

"What the hell?"

"Tell me the truth. Tell me exactly what happened the night of the accident. And don't fucking lie to me. You're one punch away from losing what few rotten teeth you have left, old man, so start talking."

Dad gets up off the sofa, albeit slowly, and tries to stand. He's drunk again, not that I find that the least bit surprising. His words are slurring and his legs are wobbly. He's a shell of the man I once knew. Hell, I wouldn't even have to punch him. One mild gust of wind and his ass would land on the floor.

"You told me on the phone *you* drove Zander and yourself home that night. A slip of the tongue, huh Dad? Zander wasn't even driving, was he?"

Silence.

"*Was he*?!" I scream, barely holding back tears, grabbing his shirt and shaking him like a fucking rag doll.

"Jesus. What difference does it make now?"

"It makes all the fucking difference. He took his own life because he thought he was the one driving. That he was the one who ran those people over on the sidewalk. He couldn't live with the guilt. But it was you, wasn't it? You were driving the car. Tell me, just how did you convince Zander he was the one driving?"

I want to kill this man. He has single-handedly ripped apart not only my family but Raina's as well.

"I don't even know what you're talkin' 'bout."

With no hesitation whatsoever, I pull back, and with all the hatred I feel right now, I land the first punch to his gut and he grunts, doubling over in agony. He deserves every bit of the pain I'm raining down on him right now.

"Shit! Okay. I was fuckin' driving. Zander came to the bar to pick me up I guess. Talked him into staying for a few beers. One led to a dozen or so, apparently. I drove us home, took the back way. Didn't even see those fucking people.

Who the hell is out walking after fucking dark anyway?" he asks as he stumbles towards the kitchen. Probably for another beer. "Zander kept saying he didn't even see them. Dumb ass didn't even realize he was in the passenger seat. Got back here, tried to drag his ass inside, but, fuck, I couldn't make it. I shoved him into the driver's seat and left him there. I came inside and passed out. I can't help it if he assumed he was the driver."

When he chuckles, my face morphs from anger to pure rage, and I can feel the blood boiling in my veins.

"You think this is funny? Zander is *dead!*" I scream as I grab him by the throat and throw him up against the living room wall. "He killed himself you son of a bitch! He thought he killed those people! But it was you all along. You took advantage of the fact that Zander was completely drunk, and you set him up." My hands are shaking as I grab his shirt and slam him against the wall again. He grunts in pain as his head jerks back, hitting the wall with force. He deserves all this pain and more for what he's done.

"I wasn't fuckin' goin' to jail!" he screams.

"So you set it up to send Zander there? You're a fucking coward is what you are. How the hell could you do that?" My fist lands a punch to the side of his face and he falls to the floor, blood pouring from his mouth. The toe of my boot connects with his side, causing him to roll to his other side, moaning in pain. "Don't you ever show your face in Hillsborough again. You come anywhere near me, and I guarantee you the cops will catch wind of this whole fucking story. You feel me, old man?"

All I make out is a grunt as I turn and storm out, tearing the screen door off the last hinge that was holding it up. Pure adrenaline is forcing me to move right now, but I don't know what the hell it is that's stopping me from killing him.

I open my car door, get inside, and think about heading

for the bar near the cheap motel where I'm staying. My mind is threatening to explode.

I can't handle this. My brother is dead, basically at the hands of my father. All he can do is laugh. All I can do is cry. Cry for the little kid I once was...the one with no mother, and a father who couldn't have cared less. I cry for my brother who felt he never had a chance in life no matter how much I tried to help him. I cry for Raina, caught in the middle of a disaster created by my family. My head falls forward hitting the steering wheel. My whole world is collapsing, and for the first time since I found my brother dead, I let go. Let the pain pull me under.

I ENTER the bar and find a seat near the back side. This place isn't too crowded so the noise isn't overbearing. I never drink, but tonight, I need to forget. I need to forget my dad, Zander, the look on Raina's face when she learned it was my twin who killed her parents. I didn't even get the whole fucking story out to tell her it wasn't Zander at all. So I'm here to forget...to drown out the memories and the anger. I order a shot of whiskey and accept the burn it creates as it slides down my throat.

"Keep them coming," I tell Jack, the bartender.

I'm suffocating, so I go back the next night, and the next, and the next.

Chapter Twenty-Six

RAINA

I'm up, wandering around my small apartment again, as rambling thoughts continue to cause sleeplessness. Standing by the window, I pull back the curtain and look out onto the quiet street. With my arms wrapped securely around my stomach, I drop my head, and I let my mind wander with thoughts of all I have lost. One lonely tear falls from the corner of my eye; that may be the only tear I have left to cry.

I think about my best friend and all that she means to me. She is really all I have left. She's called every day for the past three, and I assure her I'm fine. I'm not. I haven't left my apartment once. My emotions are at war. My thoughts are conflicting. It's hard for me to discern how I'm still so in love with the one man who has caused me such pain. The man who made me fall in love with him. The one who commanded my body and spoke to my heart. He built me up, making me feel unbreakable. Then he shattered me.

I walk back to bed, hoping to give sleep another try. There is wetness on my pillowcase from all the tears I've shed. My eyes are growing heavy from the weight of barely surviving the past three days. They close for a moment, open, and quietly close again. I finally succumb to the exhaustion, allowing my body much needed rest.

THE POUNDING at the door jars me from my sleep. I get out of bed and trudge to the door, peering through the peephole.

"Raina, open the damn door. Now."

My eyebrows raise at her command, but I open the door to keep her from bothering the neighbors, because she is damn loud.

"Okay. You're a mess. Have you seen you lately?" Sarah barges inside.

"No, I haven't. Not a beauty pageant contestant I'm guessing?" I say turning to walk towards the sofa to sit down.

"Oh, hell no! Not even close. You, my dear, have *got* to pull it together. I can't begin to imagine the hurt you feel right now, but it's time to get up and figure out how to deal with this. You can't hole up here forever. You have to start back to school tomorrow, and by the looks of you, I'd say the only thing you're ready for is...a shower. Babe, you stink. Let's go."

Sarah rushes into my bathroom and turns on the water. Knowing she won't give up and leave me alone, I follow her, pulling off my clothes as I go. I think they may just need to be burned. I'm not sure I've even changed them since Zane left.

The hot shower feels comforting as it pours over my lethargic muscles. I begin to feel slightly better, washing my hair and running conditioner through the rat's nest. The body wash smells heavenly and I am definitely feeling a little more alive and alert.

I emerge from the shower feeling a tad renewed. Sarah

has stripped the bed and put on fresh, clean sheets. The few water bottles and a solitary soda can have been thrown in the trash.

I wrap my hair in a towel and find clean clothes in the closet to put on. After drying my hair, I go out to the living room to find Sarah sitting there with a take-out order from the local diner. My stomach churns initially at the scent, but settles once I have a few refreshing sips of soda.

"You need to eat. Not much if you don't want, just eat something. And then we need to talk."

I pick at a few French fries, dipping them in ketchup, and take a small bite of the burger. It does taste good, but after days of eating barely anything, my stomach can only handle a little food. It's the soda that actually tastes the best. I put the container of food on the end table, and hold tightly to the soda, feeling as if the caffeine and sugar are a lifeline right now.

"Raina, I don't want to bring up anything that is going to upset you, but you have to know that Zane hasn't been back to work since the night he brought you home after the call from his dad. Sam is worried. He went to his apartment to check on him a few times, but he's gone, and so is his car."

"Zane's gone?" I'm not sure how I feel about this. I should be relieved, but all I can seem to feel is worry and confusion.

"Yep. Sam knocked on his door and called out to him, but there was no answer. He isn't answering his cell either. Zane's neighbor came out, I guess from all the noise, and told Sam he hasn't seen Zane at all. Do you think you need to at least try to text him or call him or something? Just to be sure he's okay. Maybe he'll answer if he knows it's you."

"No. I don't think...I can't do that."

I sit still for several minutes, my mind reeling with puzzling thoughts. I can't even make sense of all this. Sarah knows what happened, what Zane did. The lies he told.

Quite honestly, it's the police I should be calling. Zane knew his brother killed my parents, and he withheld that information. So why does she insist I call him?

"Sarah, I can't do that. I'm sorry. It just hurts too much. I'm sure he's fine. He's not mine to worry about anymore anyway," I say, trying to convince myself.

I turn and walk back into the bedroom to finish making my bed and picking up a bit, ignoring Sarah's pleas as she follows me.

"Okay. But if you hear from him, could you at least let Sam know?"

"Sure. I've got to get some things ready for school tomorrow. Can I call you later on?"

"I'm going out with Liam tonight, but call me anytime. I love you, my friend, and I'm so sorry. You'll be okay. You're stronger than you think, you know," she says, taking my hand and squeezing it.

"It's a struggle, Sarah. I just keep hoping I'll be stronger tomorrow. Go on and get ready for your date. And have fun," I say, attempting to smile. She spots the fake smile instantly.

I reach over and give Sarah a hug and she holds on tight, running her hand over the back of my head. It's comforting and gives me a tiny bit of much-needed peace. It feels good and a sense of calm washes over me, even if it's temporary.

"Talk later, babe. If you feel like it, we'll be at the bar."

"Nah. Not tonight. Some other time."

"Be sure to call me. If I don't hear from you, I'm coming back over here," she says as she heads out the door.

I am feeling somewhat thankful that she barged into my life today. I don't feel remarkably better, but baby steps. I'll just go with baby steps.

I spend the next few hours bingeing on some reality TV show that really doesn't hold my attention at all. I fix some coffee, hoping to find relaxation somewhere in that cup, and

I try reading my newest book, only to find myself rereading the same pages over and over again. I can't concentrate worth a shit.

I head to my bed, hoping for some peace. I try my best to find sleep, but all I feel is Zane. I feel his tender hands gliding like an angel's touch across my skin. I can sense his breath on my lips, and the tingling of his tongue across mine. I can feel the weight of his body as he lays on top of me. I can faintly hear him whisper how much he loves me. His scent is still on the pillow next to mine. The memories haunt me. He is everywhere and I feel as though I'm drowning in pain again, just like I did when my parents died.

Chapter Twenty-Seven

RAINA

✦✦✦

Being completely engaged in teaching first graders this past week has given me a chance to escape the pain temporarily. I'm working through my feelings and trying to rationalize why Zane would have done something like this. His words and his actions always seemed so sincere, so it's hard for me to come to terms with it all.

But something is off, and I'm not sure what it is. It's been over a week since anyone has seen or heard from him. And as crazy as it is, I'm a little worried too. Still hurt, but worried. Sam has asked Sarah again to keep him posted if I hear anything at all from Zane.

Maybe I do need to talk with him, I wonder, as I trudge up the stairs to my apartment. If for no other reason than to provide some sense of closure on our relationship. I mean, I can't continue to be with him when he hasn't been honest with me, right? No matter how sorry he seemed, or how distraught he sounded, he still kept the truth from me. He broke my trust, broke my heart.

I debated on whether to go to the police with the information. At this point, I don't know what good it will do.

Zane would have been charged with keeping these details to himself. I guess, in the end, I decide everyone has suffered enough. Zane's brother was responsible, but he is dead now too. Personally, I don't know if I can handle prying open the lid on this case, and going through all the turmoil and pain again. So I let it go. Time to move on.

I open up my apartment door, dragging my teacher bags inside with me. Laying them on the floor beside the counter, I walk into the living room and plop down in my comfy chair. I look over to the sofa, thinking of all the times we've been there, talking, cuddling, kissing. I'm trying to keep the memories at bay, but there are too many reminders. It's a noble effort, but I can't help myself. I can't think of anything but the times Zane and I were in this apartment together, and how wonderful it was. I can't help but feel his presence still here.

I get up from the chair as I hear my cell phone chiming from my purse, and I rush to answer it.

Unknown number. "Hello?"

"Is this Raina?"

"Yes, it is. Who's calling?"

"Raina, this is Jack. I'm a bartender here at The Pour House in Raleigh. There's a man here by the name of Zane. I think you know him. He's been in and out the past several days. Right now he's drunk and passed out on my office sofa."

Jesus. I can't believe Zane is drinking.

"I searched through his phone, and this was the first number in his contacts, so I called you. I think someone needs to come for him. He is really fucked up right now, and I need someone to drive over here to get him."

"Um..." I'm thinking, pacing again, and wondering what exactly I should do. "Um...yes. Okay. I can get him. I'm in

Hillsborough, though. It'll take me a little while. What's the address?"

Jack rattles off the address of the bar in Raleigh where Zane has apparently been frequenting the past few days. He doesn't drink and that concerns me. I lay my phone on top of my purse and quickly grab my overnight bag, but then I stop suddenly, frozen in place.

It hits me. His dad. Shit.

I text Sarah to let her know where I'm going and ask her to relay this to Sam. I grab a quick change of clothes and throw them in a bag, along with a few toiletries, and head out the door. Tossing the bag in the back seat, I scoot in behind the wheel and enter the address into my navigation system. I pull out, headed to Raleigh, not knowing what I'll find when I get there.

ABOUT A HALF HOUR into my drive, my cell rings. I answer, hoping it's Zane. I need to know he"s okay. I may not be seeing him anymore, and for good reason, but I certainly don't want anything bad to happen to him.

"Raina, this is Jack again. We're taking Zane to the hospital. He's unconscious. The ambulance is here now, and they've got him on the gurney, ready to transport him. They're taking him to Raleigh Memorial Hospital. Meet me there."

"Oh my God. What's happening? How much did he drink, and why the hell did you keep serving him?"

"Jesus, I didn't. He had a flask of vodka in his jacket pocket. I didn't even see it. Just meet me at the hospital. They're leaving with him now."

I end the call, my mind racing, wondering what is happening to him and why he won't wake up. For a second, I feel guilty for not letting him finish telling me what he needed to say the night he tried to explain the situation with his brother. I cut him off and sent him away.

But I can't feel guilty. He hid something from me, and it wasn't just some insignificant detail either.

I need to stop thinking about all that now and just concentrate on getting to the hospital. I call Sarah to let her know what's happening. As soon as I relay the information, she tells me she and Liam are on their way now too.

Thirty minutes later, I'm speeding through the parking lot of the hospital and luckily find a spot close to the emergency entrance. Running through the doors, I stop when I see a man waiting there.

"Raina?" he asks. My frantic look must clue him in to who I am and who I'm looking for.

"How is he? Is he awake?" My breaths come out fast from running across the parking lot.

"They took him back. The paramedic said his breathing was irregular, that it was alcohol poisoning, most likely. I don't know, Raina. I thought he would just sleep it off. He's been in a lot this week, going on about his dad and something about his brother. He kept saying "I lost her" over and over. I've been looking out for him as best I can, you know."

Oh, God.

"Has the doctor been out at all?"

"No. I've just been waiting here for you. I'll hang out here until we see how he is."

Jack guides me over to a small area with a few seats. He asks if he can get me a soda or water or something. Right now, though, the thought of putting anything in my stomach makes it churn. I'm scared, and that makes it worse.

The seats in the waiting room are as uncomfortable as shit, but we both sit here and wait. I keep my head in my hands, half bent over. He has to be okay. I feel awful because

I made him leave. I didn't even listen to him. The first thing he asked when he started to tell me what was going on, was that I listen and let him finish, so I could understand everything. And I didn't.

Zane has been abandoned in one way or another by basically everyone, just as I have. As terrible as his confession was, I should have let him finish telling me what happened. My reaction may have been exactly the same. I may have still sent him away, but at least he would have had the chance to explain.

❧

ABOUT AN HOUR AND A HALF LATER, a doctor comes out. He's an older gentleman with a fatherly looking face. Kind and gentle is how I would describe it. Jack and I stand immediately and ask if he has any information on Zane.

"I'm Dr. Malec. I've been treating Zane. Are you his wife?" he asks me, shaking my hand.

"No, I'm not. I'm his...um, his girlfriend. Raina." I hold out my hand to shake his. "He has no family except for his father who isn't available."

"Ok then. So what we're dealing with here is alcohol poisoning. We did some blood work to check his blood alcohol level. His breathing was irregular, but it's stabilizing." Dr. Malec continues to fill us in on Zane's condition and I try to stay focused. "Right now we're giving him IV fluids to prevent dehydration, and have him on oxygen."

"He'll be closely monitored as he metabolizes the alcohol and gets it out of his system. He's not out of the woods just yet, but his condition is improving slowly," he says, sounding more positive. "We'll want to get him to a regular room and out of the ER, so I'll have a nurse come out when we're ready to move him." The doctor asks if we have any

other questions and at this point, I'm just too tired to
even think.

"Thank you, Dr. Malec. I appreciate all your help."

"I'd like to ask if either of you know how often he drinks
like this?"

"Never. I've never even seen him drink. We've been
dealing with a difficult situation between us and he left about
a week ago. Jack said he's been coming into his bar quite
a bit."

"You should try to talk with him. Find out what prompted
this binge on alcohol. Alcohol poisoning can be fatal, so I
suggest he gets some help. He needs to talk to someone about
whatever is bothering him, or about whatever problems you
two are having."

"I will. And thanks again." My eyes close, and feelings of
guilt are making their way to the surface.

"The nurse will be out shortly. He'll need to be monitored
closely for a while, but when he stabilizes and they move him
to a room, you can see him."

Dr. Malec turns to walk away, but stops, pulling something out of his pocket.

"Oh, here. I think you may want this," he says, handing me
a worn, folded up piece of paper. "It was in his pants pocket
and almost fell out. I didn't open it, but I can tell it's been
read many times over. Probably important to him or something. I'd rather it not get lost."

I take the paper from him and begin to put it in my purse,
but something stops me. I pull it back out, turning it over in
my hands. It's very worn. Prominent creases. Torn edges. I'm
struggling as to what to do with this. It's Zane's, so I should
put it away and save it for him. But there is something urging
me to open it and see what's inside. So I do.

It's a note. From Zander. My stomach sinks and my heart
races. I can feel the color draining from my face as I take in

the hand-written note from Zane's twin brother. The one who killed my parents. The one who's dead.

"Jesus, Raina. You look like you've seen a ghost."

"I think I have," I say, swallowing the bile that is rising up in my throat.

At that moment, Sarah and Liam make their way into the emergency room waiting area. She grabs onto me and holds me as I fall apart yet again. We sit down together, not letting go of each other's hands. I take the note and slide it back into my bag, thankful for the interruption.

"The doctor said he should be okay. It was alcohol poisoning." I say, wiping more tears from my tired eyes.

"Shit. But he doesn't even drink. How?"

Jack tells Sarah and Liam about Zane's trips to the bar. He tells them he had a flask of vodka hidden in his jacket and they didn't realize how drunk he was until it was too late. Sarah shakes her head, tears brimming in her eyes, too.

"Why is he here in Raleigh?" Liam seems confused, and I realize that even though he plays frequently at the pub, he really doesn't know Zane all that well. In reality, no one does.

I explain to Liam that Zane is originally from Raleigh and that his father is still here. I tell him that I'm fairly certain he came here to confront his father. Liam doesn't know the entire situation, but I'm sure Sarah will eventually fill him in.

Within the next half hour, the nurse comes out to let us know they are moving Zane to a room. She tells us where to go, and we all quickly make our way to the elevator and up to the fourth floor. As we exit the elevator, my emotions begin catching up with me. The adrenaline is wearing off and I'm about to crash. Jack grabs hold of my arm and guides me to a chair in another waiting area near Zane's room.

"Just take a moment here. Sit for a minute or two. You okay?"

"Yeah. Just overwhelmed. I could use that drink now.

Liam, could you and Jack get Sarah and I something to drink, a soda or something?"

The two of them head off toward the vending machines at the end of the hallway. I take this opportunity to tell Sarah about the letter the doctor had given me that was in Zane's pocket.

"I want to read it, Sarah. I need to know."

"Are you sure? I mean, it's been an emotional day. You may want to wait a bit."

"No. I have to know."

I slowly pull the letter out of my purse and hold it gently in my hand. I hesitate, then unfold the delicate paper. I read it. Twice. More tears threaten to fall; my heart is nearly beating out of my chest. This is like a nightmare I can't wake up from. I fall back into my seat because what I read brings me to my knees.

Chapter Twenty-Eight

RAINA

Zane,

There've been so many times in my life when I've wondered why so much has happened to us. Why it was the two of us who were abandoned by Mom and left with a drunken, fucked up, father. Makes me question what the hell we ever did so wrong that we deserved that life. You were always so much better at handling that bullshit than I ever was. Always trying to make the best out of the shit hand we were dealt. You were too level-headed to let me talk you into doing the screwed up stuff I did. I guess I'm glad one of us had his head on straight. I watched alcohol take our dad from us, and ironically enough, I fell down the exact same rabbit hole.

I couldn't have asked for a better brother than you. I know I fucked up, a lot. I guess I knew deep down you'd always be there for me...to bail me out. I'm so sorry about that. You won't have to bail me out again. And you're better off for that.

You already know about Raina. Watch over her, man. I took her parents from her, and I don't even deserve to breathe the same air she does. I don't deserve to breathe at all. Keep your distance, because our family shit doesn't have any place in her life. Just make sure she's safe.

I love you, Z-man. You're the best. Take care of yourself and live a good life.

Zander

GUILT. Suicide.

Zander committed suicide.

Oh, God. Zane. His twin brother didn't just die.

He killed himself. He killed himself out of guilt for killing my parents, and he wanted Zane to watch over me. Could this situation possibly get any more fucked up? No wonder Zane was so indifferent toward me at the pub before we got together. I reminded him of the very reason his brother was dead, the reason why Zander took his own life. And yet, he did everything he could to help me. So compassionate and selfless.

Closing my eyes, I try to shake off the messy feelings. I stand and begin an unsettled pace back and forth in the hospital waiting room, the hand holding the letter shaking with an uneasiness that causes my stomach to swirl. I sit again, hoping to quickly put some of this into perspective before I see Zane.

If I thought my insides were twisted before, I can't put into words the confusion swirling through my mind right now. This shitstorm has turned my emotions into a chaotic mess. It's an inner battle that I need to wrestle with in order to move forward...whether that's with or without Zane.

I need some answers.

"Raina?" I faintly hear Sarah's voice as I'm folding up the letter.

"Um...yeah. I'd like to go in to see Zane now," I stammer.

"Are you okay? You're not looking too good right now."

"I'm good. I'm good. Just..."

"The letter?" Sarah asks.

I wave her off and tell her it was nothing of importance. If Zane ever wants anyone to know his brother committed suicide, he'll tell them. It's not my place or my story to tell. But, right now I need to get into his room. I need to see him. And I hope that when I lay eyes on him, my emotions will untangle themselves and my choices become clear. I can only hope.

Chapter Twenty-Nine

ZANE

य

My eyes are heavy and I keep trying to open them. What is that constant beeping? Damn, I feel like I was run over by a truck. *Whose voice is that? Rain? Is that you?* I try to move, to pull myself out of this fog, but it's so hard. Where the hell am I?

After a few minutes of struggling, I open my eyes slowly, then blink quickly, in an attempt to focus on whoever is sitting near me.

Raina.

"You're awake. Oh, thank God." Raina's here and I reach for her hand. She quickly stands and is by my side immediately. At that moment, I see a nurse and a doctor moving quickly into the room. Shit. I've landed myself in the hospital. Memories begin to surface. The bar, the flask of vodka. Drunk. I was drunk. How did I end up here?

"Zane. I'm Dr. Malec. How are you feeling?" he asks, reaching for my hand.

My stomach is churning, my head is pounding like a fucking hammer, and my throat feels like sandpaper. "Like shit."

"Do you have any recollection of what happened to you?"

"I was at a bar. I was talking to the bartender. Drinking a lot. Too much, apparently."

"You think right," Dr. Malec says. "You were rushed in here, unconscious, with alcohol poisoning. You're lucky to be alive. We've got some IV fluids in you now. I'm going to take off the oxygen tube in a few hours. We'll keep you through the night just to monitor you," he explains. "You're going to be fine, but you sure gave everyone a scare." He pats my leg as the nurse continues to check my vital signs. He's an older man who reminds me of a very kind teacher I had in high school. The one who knew about my home situation and did his best to help me with my schoolwork so I wouldn't fall behind. He was always looking out for me. "The nurse will be in to check on you in a bit." Dr. Malec turns to leave my room.

I look at Raina and see my angel. She stands by my side like a guardian, and I hope against hope she's here to forgive me. God, I've missed her. "I'm so sorry. I didn't mean for this to happen. How did you get here?"

Raina drops her head and fuck, if I don't hate that. She tells me that the bartender called her, got her number from my phone and called her to ask for help.

My mind rings with confusing thoughts, one of which is why Raina came here for me after what I did. I'll take her forgiveness, if, in fact, she's offering it, even though I absolutely don't deserve it.

"Zane, there was a note in your pocket. The doctor gave it to me."

Oh shit. Zander's note.

The somber look on Raina's face is very telling. She read the note, and she knows.

"Why didn't you tell me, Zane? You said Zander was dead.

Why didn't you tell me what really happened?" she whispers, leaning toward me.

I think about that question and can't really come up with an answer. I guess I just didn't want her to see how my life spiraled out of control, and I didn't want to relive that tragedy all over again. Raina has her own adversities to overcome. I guess I didn't want to add to it.

"I wanted to help *you*. You're the most important thing to me. You have to know that. I wanted to comfort you and protect you. I can handle my own shit. I just wanted to help you handle yours."

And that is the God's honest truth. I want to be there for her, every waking moment, and hold her every night while we sleep.

"Well, as evidenced by tonight's debacle, you really aren't handling things at all." She has a point. Although this mess has less to do with Zander's death and everything to do with my dad.

I study her face and her body language for a sign. Any sign that maybe all hope isn't lost. I have more to tell her, but I'm too exhausted to get into it right now. We will talk though, and she will know every fucked up side of this story before it's all said and done. After seeing my dad when I returned to Raleigh, I know for certain that, while he may still be breathing, he is dead to me. His actions and his lies have solidified that.

"The doctor says you'll be released tomorrow. I don't know if it's a good idea or not, but, I can stay here in Raleigh and drive you back to Hillsborough tomorrow...unless you're not planning to go back, that is. Whatever you want. I don't know about your car. Just a thought." She's still standing by my side and I begin to feel some sense of relief.

She gives me a tentative smile, and that's all I need. She's not completely gone, and I sense a slight crack in her armor.

This may be the opportunity that I need to win her back and I'm determined to do just that. I want Raina forever, and this time, no lies, no half-truths. Just us. Honesty and trust. After spending the last several days in a drunken stupor, in a fog, everything is crystal fucking clear to me right now.

"I'd like that. I need to get out of this town for good. There's nothing left here for me." I close my eyes and shake my head, wondering if what I want to say next will be well received.

"I want to be where you are, Raina. I need to fix this."

"Zane, don't. I can't do this right now. I'll be back tomorrow to get you. If you want, I can go to wherever you were staying and get your things."

She said she can't do this *now*, which means we will revisit this whole mess later. She needs to know that I'm not giving up. Her resolve is no match for my determination. Right now I'm more than determined than ever to get her back.

I explain to Raina where to get the few things I brought with me and where to take the motel key. Once I leave this hospital and head back to Hillsborough, I won't be coming back.

Raina takes my hand and gently squeezes it. "I really am glad you're okay. Physically, anyway. I think we both need to get some things worked out emotionally, though. We're both kind of a mess," she says. I have to admit that she is spot on, but there is no doubt we will work things out. On our own, *and* with each other, because there is no other option for me.

Chapter Thirty

RAINA

I wake up slowly and sit up in bed after a restless night's sleep. Thinking of Zane, his dad, my parents, and especially Zander kept me from sleeping through the night. So many emotions are coming out to play right now, that it is physically exhausting. Never, in my wildest dreams, did I ever consider that this is the path my life would have taken. That I would fall in love with the one man who had the power to bring me to my knees. And then did exactly that. It's as though I've fallen into some alternate universe where I'm sitting on the outside looking in at the tragedy that is my life.

The free coffee in the hotel room isn't anything to write home about, but it's coffee, so it'll have to do. I stand by the window and look out over the city. I remember so many things about my life here. I know it will never be the same without my parents, and I've been working towards accepting that, but this situation with Zane has caused me to reexamine so many things.

I'm trying to establish whether or not he came to me out of pity or whether his feelings for me are genuine. He's spoken to me at times with such passion and with such sincerity, that it's hard to imagine his feelings for me are anything but authentic. It will eventually come down to following my instincts. I'll talk with Zane, and I believe my heart will lead me in the right direction. Following my heart hasn't necessarily worked out for me in the past, but it's time to just be in the present, to stop obsessing, stop over-thinking, and stop what-iffing things to death. Just trust my journey and the path I'm on. Trust that whatever is meant to be, will be. Trust that my mind will hear my intuition over my fear.

The warmth of the water in the shower relieves some of the knots building in my muscles. It also causes memories of my time with Zane in the shower to resurface, and I smile and blush all over again. After getting out of the shower, I use the towel to wipe off the steam that has built up on the mirror, and I look at myself for a long time. I look tired, yet I see resilience in my eyes.

With my hair pulled back in a ponytail, donning clean clothes, I make my way to the car, ready to pick up Zane. There's a chilly wind blowing as I toss my bags into the car. The sun is no longer shining. The thick clouds overhead hint at another dreary winter day.

On the way to the hospital, I take a slight detour and end up at the cemetery where my parents are buried. I haven't been here in a long time and part of me feels bad about that. I know Mom and Dad, though, and they wouldn't be upset about that at all. But, it's time.

I drive slowly along the single lane road to the area in the back lot where they're buried. It takes me a few minutes to get out of the car, but eventually, I do. I hear a few birds chirping from the nearby trees, as I put my mittens on and walk over to their grave. I bet they're struggling through these short, cold days of winter too. But other than those few birds, this place is relatively silent. I take a few minutes to wipe away some brush and fallen leaves from my parents' headstones. Standing again, I zip my coat and wrap my scarf tightly around my neck to ward off the chill in the winter air. Using the sleeve of my coat, I wipe the tears from my eyes and try to gather some strength.

"Hey. It's me. Of course, I'm sure you know that. I miss you both so very much. Things here are all mixed up right now and my head is all over the place. I wish you were here to talk to, but I guess if you were here, I would have never met Zane. God, even saying that feels twisted.

"We've been seeing each other for a while now. Funny how things happen. I found out, though, that his brother is the one who hit you that night. He was drunk. He and Zane had a really hard life so his brother drank a lot. Zane knew about the accident, but he kept it from me and I have no idea why. I don't think I'll ever forgive his brother for doing what he did. But Zane. He's so broken right now. I don't really know what to do. I still love him, I do know that much. I just don't know how to get over what he did.

"There's so much to figure out it kinda makes my head spin. I remember you used to say that I made your head spin sometimes when I was little. You always said I had so much energy and wouldn't ever slow down. Ironically, I teach a lot of kids just like that now."

I laugh a little to myself thinking about the kids I teach, as well as my life as a child. I take a minute to wipe away more tears. The more I talk about everything, the more focused and clear my mind becomes. Kneeling down, I lightly run my hand over the grass, remembering. I stand back up, knowing I have to leave soon.

"I guess, deep down, I know Zane didn't keep the truth from me to hurt me. He isn't that kind of person. I think you'd like him. Even you, Dad. He works hard and we've spent a lot of fun times together. When I'm with him, I'm just happy. I think I need to find it in my heart to forgive him. Maybe doing that will help."

I stand there for a few more minutes, my arms wrapped around my body for comfort, as a few stray tears make their way down my cheeks. Then, for this single moment in time, the sunshine peeks through the ominous clouds, and rays of light shine down like a beacon, brightening up the headstone where my parents' names are etched. The light sweeps across the grass covering their graves and I instantly feel the warmth. As quick as the sun comes out, though, it disappears, but it leaves me with a sense of comfort and calm, like the comfort I always felt when Mom and Dad were still alive. Looking back to the sky, I smile.

Before I leave, I promise them that I'll be back. I take a deep breath and turn to walk back to my car. I need to get to Zane.

I got his message while I was driving, to let me know he was being discharged. I pull into the parking lot and take a few minutes to center my thoughts. I look up toward the heavens where I know Mom and Dad are looking down and watching over me. At that moment, it occurs to me that all the times Zane has looked up at the sky, he was doing the same thing I was. His mind was focused on Zander. His twin.

We've both lost so much. And with everything out in the open now, maybe we can find our way together. Those thoughts help me to come to terms with the fact that I have to forgive Zane so that my own soul can find some peace.

❧

I walk into his room, and I can hear Zane fussing at the nurses as they try to get him into the wheelchair. He's insisting on walking, but that won't happen with these two drill sergeants. He finally gives up and sits down as the doctor comes into his room.

"Dr. Malec, hello."

"I just came in to talk for a minute." He nods to the nurses and they exit the room as Zane remains in the wheelchair. "Zane, you had a close call, son. I hope you realize how fortunate you are. Some people in those same circumstances don't get a second chance." Second chances. Funny he should say that, because that's exactly what my heart wants. "There's a counselor I know well in Hillsborough. Here's his card. Use it. Work through whatever you need to. This young lady here obviously wants to see you well. See to it you get there."

"Thank you, sir."

"Take care of yourself. And young lady, you see to it he does just that."

I smile at Dr. Malec and thank him for being so good to Zane, then shake his hand as the two nurses walk back into the room. One nurse pushes Zane out of the room, and we make our way to the exit. I hurry out of the exit first and walk to the car to bring it around to the main door to get Zane.

Once he's settled in the car, Zane puts his hand on my thigh, causing me to glance his way, but I don't make him move it. He's searching for some answers right now. I know he wants to know what happens from here. I put the car in drive and head toward his car at the motel, so that we can get it to drive home. He is insistent that he'll never come back to Raleigh, but Zander is buried here too, so I hope one day he'll return for that reason. He'll figure it out. It's a lot to sort through for him right now.

I pull into the motel lot beside Zane's car. He turns and with a touch of happiness in his voice he says, "I'll follow you. You may not be able to keep up if I lead." He says smiling. Then he hesitates, and his voice turns more serious. "Raina..."

"We'll talk when we get home," I say, smiling.

"Yeah. When we get home. Would you be okay if I came to your apartment?"

"How about tomorrow? It's been a long two days."

Zane forces a smile. "Sure, tomorrow. Coffee at the coffee shop?"

"How about coffee at my place?"

"I'll be there at ten. Be ready to talk Raina. I have to get everything out in the open. I want to rebuild what we have. I know I've messed this up, but you need to know I intend to do all I can possibly do to fix this. Fix us. For me, there is no other choice." He smiles as he leans across the console and his open palm finds its way to my neck, his thumb caressing my cheek. "I don't think you are any match for my determination right now, sweetheart." I can't help but lean into it and close my eyes, as my insides turn to jelly. I don't want to admit it, but his touch is healing my soul. It's my Heaven.

"Drive safe, angel."

Zane takes his hand away from my face and instantly I feel the loss. He gets out of my car, closing the door, and pounds twice on the top. I look through the side window and see him leaning down, and his hand shows his thumb, his pointer finger and his pinky all raised...the sign for I love you.

I love you too.

Chapter Thirty-One

ZANE

Raina follows me back to Hillsborough, and the drive seems much longer and more tedious than normal. I know it's because this conversation with Raina is going to happen much sooner than I'd imagined. When I left for Raleigh, I honestly believed we were over. I broke the trust between us. It takes time to build trust between two people, and I shattered it in a matter of minutes. In my mind, the heartbreak I caused her may have created a chasm between us that can never be bridged. So the fact that she is even talking to me is a miracle in itself.

I follow Raina to her apartment and help her get her bag from the back seat. Handing it to her, I convince myself that I need to give her this time, this night, to come to terms with everything that has happened over the past week. I pray she doesn't over think everything, because if she does, she may very well put an end to our relationship. She may convince herself that she can no longer trust me, that what I kept from her is too much of a personal burden to overcome. Not that I would blame her in the least.

To say all this shit has put a strain on my nerves is the

understatement of the year. Right now I'm walking a very fine line between wanting to give her time to herself and tossing her over my shoulder, taking her to her apartment and showing her in every way I can think of that I love her.

"So, I'll see you tomorrow?" she asks timidly as she turns to me.

"Absolutely. Get some rest," I say, pulling her into me and wrapping her in my arms. I gently place a kiss on top of her head, with as much love and emotion possible, so she feels my strength, my resolve, and my commitment to her. This is where she belongs. No one else but her.

Her hands instinctively grasp the back of my shirt. I can feel her breathing and her heart begin to race. She's feeling so many conflicting emotions right now, and I don't want her to be any more unsettled with me than she already is. The best thing I can do for her is to pull back a little, no matter how hard it is. I take a step back and hand her the bag.

Raina takes it and makes her way inside. I lean against my car, crossing my feet, my hands in my pockets, and wait for her to get inside. Her door shuts, and I know it will be tomorrow before I see her again.

I get into my car just as it begins to rain. Even the damn weather is depressing.

My apartment has been empty for over a week now, so I hit the grocery store on the way home for a few things. I left so impulsively that I don't even remember turning off the lights.

With groceries and my duffle bag in tow, I head into my apartment. I drop the bag near the sofa and put the groceries away, feeling completely exhausted. Looking around this place, I think back on all that has happened. It's hard to believe that this is my life. A mother who is God only knows where. A father that...well, I no longer consider that man my father. A real father would never be physically and mentally abusive. A real father would never devalue the life of his son to the point that he sets him up for a possible manslaughter or even murder charge, then laughs at his death. The thought still infuriates me, so I try to put it out of my mind altogether.

There are times when my brother's loss is so great that is difficult to endure. But it's in those times that I remember Raina and the struggle she has experienced. Still experiencing, really. She is so strong, the strongest, most beautiful woman I know, and if she finds it in her heart to forgive me, I will spend every waking second of my life making it up to her. She deserves no less than that.

I pull out the card that Dr. Malec gave me and lay it on the counter. Maybe this is where I start.

Chapter Thirty-Two

RAINA

Waiting for Zane to show up is like waiting for a tornado. You know it's coming and may very well destroy everything in its path as it surges through. Sounds dramatic, I know.

There is a knock at the door. The storm has arrived. I just hope I can come out of it relatively unscathed.

I open the door as casually as I can fake and there he stands, all tall and beautiful, leaning against the framework of the door. With one leg crossed over the other, and arms folded, his eyes dance in amusement when he notices my eyes making their way up and down his body. But, damn. He fills the doorway with his presence, and I step back to take it all in. Worn jeans, hanging low on his hips, a fitted long-sleeved tee, damp hair styled, but not, so it looks just perfect. My breathing shallows just a touch.

Get your shit together, Raina.

He steps forward, inching closer to me with every move-ment. He dips low and cradles his hand around my neck. The smell of this man is intoxicating, and he becomes even more irresistible when his lips brush against my cheek in the sweetest of kisses.

"Hello, angel."

Jesus.

I take a breath and will myself to step back away from the tension that is building between us. He isn't going to fight fair, I can see that for certain.

"Zane, hey. So...come on in. I mean, you're already in...so...never mind."

He chuckles and makes his way to the counter, where he leans against it, waiting for me to catch up. Which is unlikely, considering the way he just swaggered into my apartment. His tight fitting tee rides up slightly when he crosses his arms in front of his chest.

"Coffee?" I ask.

"Of course."

He walks to the sofa and takes a seat. Coffees in hand a few minutes later, I sit at one end of the sofa, which doesn't leave a tremendous amount of room, as Zane has seen fit to sit directly in the middle.

"How are you feeling?" I ask, as I hand him his coffee. It makes me smile to know he is cultivating this coffee habit all for me.

"Much better, actually. Physically, anyway." And I agree. The color is back in his face and his smile has returned. "After seeing my dad, things spiraled out of control quickly. The situation with Zander isn't exactly what I thought and I lost it. It started out as just a drink to lessen the sting of what I had learned. The more I drank, the more I forgot, and the better I felt."

"What happened when you saw your dad?" I'm not sure I truly want to hear this part of the story, but I know Zane wants everything out in the open, so I have to let him explain. I sit still and wait for a moment, letting him get prepared to clarify this mess for me. He runs his hands through his hair a few times, then settles.

"The situation with my brother and what happened with your parents isn't exactly what really went down that night."

The suffocating feeling is bubbling up around me again. I can feel my hands begin to shake.

"When Dad called me at the bar last week, he was drunk. Started spewing bullshit about me not being there for him and needing money. All bullshit. He's never contacted me until now, and I didn't want all that interfering with us. He rambled on, and said that he...I had hoped to God that I'd heard him wrong." Zane stops and lowers his head, putting his face in his hands, silent for a few seconds.

"Angel, Dad was the one driving the car that killed your parents."

This can't be happening.

The look of shock must scare him enough to move quickly, because before I can even take a step, he's right beside me, hands on my face, his forehead touching mine. Both our eyes are rimmed with tears.

"God, angel. I'm so sorry. I didn't know. Dad and Zander were both drunk and when they finally made it to Dad's driveway, he tried to get Zander to the house. He couldn't get any further than the driver's door with him. He opened the door and pushed him into the seat, left him passed out there until the next morning. Zander assumed he'd been driving. He barely remembered the accident. He just knew two people were hit by the car he was in. Dad never told him otherwise. Just let him believe he killed them. It's a fucking train wreck."

I'm stunned, appalled that a father would do something so heinous to his own son, his own flesh and blood. "All this time your dad knew? And Zander. God, I'm so sorry!"

"Jesus, Rain. My dad killed your parents. Why the hell

should you be sorry?" He stands and begins pacing back and forth, with a little frustration and a whole lot of confusion on his face, eyes wild with fury and rage.

"I know. But Zander. All the guilt he felt? He never got over it, and he hadn't even done anything to feel guilty about. And now he's gone. How could your dad do something that evil?" I am so completely and utterly pissed right now, it's hard to think. I grab onto Zane, wanting something to ground me after hearing this.

"Who the fuck knows. He was a shit dad from the time Mom left us. We were an inconvenience to him. I left here that night, after I told you what I knew, or what I thought I knew, and when I got to Raleigh, I went straight to his house. I basically cut loose and beat the shit out of him. I told him never to look for me or call me again, or I'd be sure the police were given enough information so they would come looking for him. What I really want is to speak with the police anyway and tell them everything. He needs to pay for what he's done to you. But more than that, you deserve to have some closure."

I sit still, barely moving after hearing this new information. I told you. Tornado.

If Zane goes to the police, and it sounds like that's precisely what he wants to do, I'm certain that he will end up charged with something because of withholding information about the accident, even though his information wasn't true. He's going to risk possibly going to jail, so that I can have some sense of closure with this whole mess, and maybe to clear his conscience as well. I would love to see his dad arrested and put in jail for the rest of his pathetic life for what he did to my family. But, Zane was caught in this middle of this storm, and he's been through hell.

I know we've got a long way to go and a lot of knots to untangle in our relationship, but I can't even consider the idea of Zane getting into trouble. The fact that he lost his brother, then discovered his dad was the driver, has *got* to be punishment enough. I don't know how he can even make sense of all this.

"No. You don't go to the police. I mean it, Zane. I really do. Yes, it was wrong of you not to tell me what you knew, and I'm trying to understand the reasons why you didn't. You've punished yourself enough for a situation that was completely out of your control. No one wants to see your dad suffer any more than me, but at some point, this nightmare has to come to an end."

"That means my dad goes unpunished. Can you live with that? Because I don't know how *I* can live with that." His troubled eyes and sharp, jittery movements indicate a tremendous amount of anger toward his father, and rightfully so. I feel that same resentment toward him, but in my mind, I want this all to be over.

"What good would it do? You said yourself that he's a drunk, and he's barely surviving. He doesn't have much of a life as it is. Honestly, I don't feel the least bit sorry for him. But we have a chance to put this all behind us right now."

Zane's hands come to my face and he stares at me with such concentration, like he's reaching down into my soul.

"How are you even real? After everything that's happened, you're still willing to try to forgive me."

"Zane, I'm willing to talk more. Coming to terms with everything that's happened between us will be hard. Forgiveness isn't always an easy thing, but I'm trying to put myself in your place, and I'm hoping to understand the choices you made." I try to turn away from him, but he holds firm, not letting me go.

"I don't deserve an ounce of your forgiveness, sweetheart. I know that. I can give you tons of reasons why I did what I did, but they're just that. Reasons...not excuses. There is no excuse for keeping the truth from you."

"My mind and my heart need peace right now. I have to let some of this mess go. I love you, Zane. I really do. I want us to get to a point where all this is just a bad memory. I want to be able to trust you again."

"I'll show you every day for the rest of my life how much you mean to me and how much you can trust me. I just need a chance. Please tell me you can give me that, baby."

I look at him. *Really* and truly look at him.

"Complete honesty, Zane. I can't go through this again."

Zane pulls back but says nothing. He looks at me with determination, but most of all love. There is a silent connection between us. An understanding of sorts. I know that Zane will do all he can to prove to me that I can trust him again. It will take some time, most definitely, but I have to be able to trust him again. And I need to trust myself. I don't want to question my feelings anymore.

"You'll see, angel. You are worth more to me than anything. You're the very best part of me, baby. My better half. And I love you so much."

Conviction resonates in his words. So much so, I can't deny that what he is saying is the truth. He certainly has a generous and tender heart for a man having grown up without parents to show him what pure and honest love looks like.

Chapter Thirty-Three

ZANE

❧

Raina and I spend the rest of the day together. Opening up a little more about my mother isn't high on the list of what I want to talk about today, but Raina needs to trust that I will be completely open with her. I don't remember a lot about my mom, but what memories I have of her, I share.

"Your eyes soften when you talk about her and your voice is quieter and steady. It's easy to see that she was an important part of your life, even for the short time she was with you"

"I've never tried to find her. I don't know if that makes me a bad son or not. When I think of her, all I feel is the loss, like she just abandoned me. Like she didn't love me. It's painful and in some ways, still raw. Sometimes it feels like it was just yesterday she walked out on us."

I have so many unanswered questions surrounding my mother's absence that it's difficult to think about. It's hard not to let myself fall apart right now. I feel like a man who basically hit rock bottom, and endured some of the worst life can dish out. Strength and tenacity are qualities that I know will help me come back from all this. I'm determined to continue to make a respectable life for myself.

Raina's hand covers mine in comfort. "I can't pretend to understand your kind of loss. I'm sure there's a reason why she left. You might never know, but I can imagine if she were here right now, she would be proud of the compassionate and kind man you are. Especially knowing that you really raised yourself."

"She might be. Who knows?"

What I do know is that I'm ready to wrap up this depressing discussion and get the hell out of here for a while.

§◆

WE MAKE our way down to the coffee shop. It's kind of like our place now. I think back to that day, to when our relationship first began. We've been through so much in such a short amount of time.

Our regular table is open and we head over to sit down. I take Raina's hand in mine, rubbing my thumb gently along her soft skin.

"I want you to know that before I came to your apartment this morning I made a call to the therapist Dr. Malec recommended. I'm going to start some sessions with him next week. I think it's really going to be good for me."

Smiling, Raina leans over and kisses my cheek. "I think so too."

"I loved my brother, and he's gone, and I miss him. So damn much. But I also feel guilty about hating him for the situation he put both of us in. It's confusing and depressing to feel like that."

In my mind, I'm not sure I hate Zander. Actually, I'm unsure of how I should feel about anything. Giving voice to my emotions isn't that easy, since I've had basically no one to listen to me or validate my feelings for basically my entire life. The only feeling that I'm confident about right now is that I love Raina. Maybe that's all that matters.

"It isn't any wonder you feel like that. It was a tenuous position to be put in, and I can't blame you for feeling confused and angry."

"I can tell you that it made me feel better just making the call. I want to show you that I mean what I say. That I'm willing to do all I can to make this relationship work."

"I think that's a wonderful first step, and the right thing to do. And I'll be with you every step of the way. If I've learned anything from the past few years, Zane, it's that healing takes time. And healing from this means forgiving yourself for your mistakes. Give yourself time to take all those broken pieces and put them together again."

"You're sexy when you're all philosophical, babe." Those eyebrows wiggle up and down again. I know humor is Zane's way of dealing with difficult conversations, so I just laugh with him and let it go.

"Seriously though, I told him a little about our relationship, and he suggested that at some point you could join in on our time. But only if you want to. I hope I didn't overstep. I just thought he should know everything about how...unconventionally our relationship started." He shakes his head and lets out a grunt.

I take a second to think about that, and decide that joining him in his sessions may be the best thing for us. If we really want our relationship to work, we need to take this opportunity to build a more solid foundation so that we can build a strong life together.

"I think that's a great idea."

Chapter Thirty-Four

ZANE

The following weekend, Raina comes with me to the bar since I'm scheduled to work. I am so grateful to Sam for holding on to my job for me. I know I left him in a bind when I went off the radar for a while, but that's just the kind of guy he is.

Sarah comes in late to the bar and sidles up beside Raina. The two drink their wine and giggle like schoolgirls catching up on town gossip. Since Raina's been spending most of her time with me, they haven't seen each other much outside of school. And it seems that Sarah has been spending more time with Liam, although she's doing her best to convince us they're just friends. I, however, see the look in Liam's eyes when he catches sight of her, and that is definitely not a look a man gives his friend. He wants a hell of a lot more than friendship from her.

Throughout the night, Raina's eyes frequently find mine, and when she looks at me, all I see is her beautiful smile. It's all I can do to stay behind the bar and not drag her back to the office.

Liam and Cole are playing again tonight, so I asked Liam

earlier if he would play a special song for my girl. When I hear the first few notes of Raina's favorite Ed Sheeran song, I reach across the bar and take her hand, pulling her to the dance floor. I hold her closely, running my hand up and down her back. Her body relaxes and melts into mine, her head resting gently on my chest. Holding on to her like this is one of those moments that I will always remember. Raina really does look perfect tonight. She's my angel and she's mine.

🕊

As the evening winds down, Raina helps me clean the bar area and lock up. Her apartment is where we've been spending most of our time, so we head back there for the night.

I've been hesitant to initiate sex between us because I want her to know I am serious about our relationship and rebuilding the trust between us. Reliving her parents' death was very hard on her, to say the least. The fact that she's forgiven me is actually a miracle in my eyes. Her forgiveness won't ever change what happened in the past, but it has changed my future. My future is with her. Tonight, I'm going to show her in every way I can, that she is mine.

We make it through the door and I toss my keys on her counter. In no time, I have her lifted up, and I anxiously carry her to the bed. If there is an ounce of skepticism when I look in her eyes, I'll stop this immediately.

When my eyes meet hers, though, I see nothing but heat and excitement. She knows where this is going.

"Close your eyes, angel. But keep your heart open," I say, as I cover her beautiful body with mine. I lean close to her, kissing her neck, and whisper, "I love you Rain. I love your smile, your touch, your mind, your soul. Everything that makes you who you are. Nothing will keep me away from you ever again."

After I can no longer stand to keep my hands off her, they begin to work agonizingly slow to remove her clothing piece by piece. I can feel her struggling to maintain some kind of control. She's trying to reach for me, but I gently take both her hands and pin them to her sides. She's mine to savor, to love.

I realize that I'm holding on by a thread, but my girl deserves patience and love. She's forgiven what I deemed unforgivable. And now she's mine, lying here naked, beautifully naked. Her creamy, delicate skin tingles at my touch, and her smile is so bright right now, the light from the sun in the afternoon sky suffers by comparison.

With my clothes removed, I crawl back onto the bed and cover her gorgeous body again with mine. Flesh on flesh, we lose ourselves in a sensual kiss as our hands feather over every inch of each other's skin. My erection nestled against her stomach becomes almost painful. My hand caresses the heat between her legs as her breathing becomes choppy, and I feel the sudden wetness that hints at her readiness for me.

Taking my aching cock in my hand, I spread her legs gently, then slide into her, into heaven. She is absolute perfection.

My movements begin slowly, savoring every sweet part of her. Sex with Raina is more than just sex. This right here is the definition of making love. It's as though she's showing me the very essence of her. Every thought in her mind and every feeling in her soul. I am one lucky son-of-a-bitch.

Raina's hands pull at my back and her fingernails scratch with need. Her hips begin to thrust upwards more quickly, which is a tell-tale sign she's nearing orgasm. I'm buried so deep inside her right now, I may never come out again. This is pure, unadulterated heaven.

"Zane. Oh, God. Zane. Please..."

I can't hold back, it's too much.

"Take me, angel. Take all of me. I need it hard, baby. Hold on."

Her legs pull up so that her knees are close to her shoulders. I pin her hands over her head and pound into her delicious heat with strength and passion as she moans those sweet, sexy sounds. Sweat begins to bead on my forehead, and I continue to thrust fiercely, engraining myself into her soul. This feeling is the best high, the best drunk...all without taking a hit or a drink. She is intoxicating.

Soon, she begins to fall apart, and I feel her insides begin to quiver. I try to prolong the inevitable, but it's no use. I'm unable to keep my orgasm at bay, and I come hard as she falls over the edge magnificently, releasing the breath she was holding. Her panting breaths mimic mine.

We lay still, holding onto each other. We're spent. Physically, emotionally spent. Completely lost in the moment with each other.

I roll to my back, taking Raina with me so she's spread across my chest. My hands drift toward her face and I feel the wetness on her cheeks. I struggle to sit up and pull her closer to me.

"Baby, what's wrong? Oh, shit. Are you hurt? Did I hurt you?"

"No, Zane. You didn't hurt me. You put me back together."

Chapter Thirty-Five

RAINA

I'm not exactly sure at what point I fell asleep in the early morning hours, but I am awakened by the sound of my cell phone. I reach over top of Zane and grab my phone to see that it's Sarah. I send it to voicemail, deciding to talk to her later. After last night, I feel like today is just for Zane and me. It's been a long road, no doubt about it, but I can feel that strong connection between us again.

Having said that, I admit that I'm still a little worried about Zane. He's kept so many things bottled up inside for so long. I will certainly be there for him when he needs me, but I know he will benefit from talking with the therapist he's called. He needs to heal and learn to overcome all the anger and guilt that I know he feels.

I crawl out of bed and grab Zane's tee to put on. Feeling parched, I get a glass of water and quickly shoot a text to Sarah, letting her know everything is okay and that I'll catch up with her later.

I go back into the bedroom and stare at the man taking up almost all of my bed. Makes me wonder how there's any room for me. The sheet barely covers him from the waist down, which puts those rippled abs on full display. The small line of happy trail hair is visible and reminds me of where that beautiful trail leads. I smile and blush just a little at that thought.

"Sweetheart, you really do have to stop staring so much. I'm getting a complex," he says without opening his eyes.

"Not likely, babe. Have you seen you?" I say jokingly.

Zane laughs out loud, then leans over to check his watch in the pocket of his jeans laying on the floor. And sweet Jesus, there goes the sheet. "Shit. We slept till almost dinner time. You worked me over good, babe, and fucking exhausted me."

My hand comes up to my mouth to stifle a grin. "You're in *my* bed, naked, grumbling about how I worked *you* over? After you went all caveman on me last night, I may never walk right again."

Zane gets up, completely naked, and grabs my hand, pulling me into his chest. "If I have anything to say about it, you never will. I could live inside you, babe."

"Well, I don't think that's a good idea, since I have to teach on Monday. Might make things a little awkward at work, don't you think?" I say, as I reach up to kiss him.

"What I think is that you should make yourself useful and fetch me some food, wench. Your man is starved," he says with a smile.

"Then nourishment it is, good sir. I shall utilize the communication services available and arrange delivery of some of the town's finest cuisine," I reply with a bow.

We both begin laughing and stand there together for just a moment more, Zane's arms wrapping tightly around me, his chin on my head.

"I love you, baby. You have no idea how much it means that you've forgiven me. I really made some bad decisions and almost ruined everything."

"But you didn't ruin everything. No more apologies. Let's just learn from all that's happened and look forward, okay?"

Zane leans down, placing both hands on my face. "I love you, Raina. More than I could have ever imagined loving anyone in my entire life. I want you and me. And I want it forever."

To have Zane's lips tangled up with mine makes me the luckiest woman in the world. His tongue skims across the plumpness of my lips and his thumbs gently caress my cheeks. as my heart skips a beat. My body succumbs to his kiss. The kiss that convinces me, once and for all, that my life is complete with him.

He pulls back slightly. "Forever."

Epilogue

ZANE

I t's been a little over six months since I confessed to Raina that I had been keeping the truth about her parents' accident from her. At least what I *thought* was the truth anyway. We've been working with a counselor - sometimes together, sometimes separately - ever since. She has thrived in those sessions, and has worked through so much grief that she tried to ignore for so long. I've never seen her so happy and it soothes my heart to watch her shine.

There were moments, though, during the whole process, where I could see so much pain in her eyes and hear such sadness in her voice as she talked about how much she missed them. It hurt knowing my family had something to do with all that grief. These were the biggest concerns I always voiced to my therapist. Trying to let go of the guilt was no easy task.

I've finally managed to open up about my abusive father, and Zander's suicide too. I've accepted that I played no part in my father's mental demise, nor my brother's suicide, and coming to that realization has helped me tremendously. Doubt creeps back into my mind every now and then, but having someone to talk with makes those feelings so much easier to manage. It took a while to bring it all to light, but I never realized how much of an effect those feelings had in every facet of my life. Understanding that has allowed me to heal and to let go of so much pain I had held on to.

We talk a lot about my mother as well. I'll never understand what caused her to leave Zander and me with my dad, but again, it's not something I can change unless I look for her. Right now, I don't want that. I just want to heal with my girl and make a life with her. She's my family. She is home.

We've let my apartment go, and I've been living with her for the past month. Waking up to her beautiful smile every morning is like an addiction. I don't think I'll ever get enough. I make her coffee as she gets ready for her school day, and we eat dinner together every evening before I head to the bar.

My nights at the pub can be long, but she usually stops by for at least a little while to keep me company while I work, taking her usual seat. I like tending bar, but I know it isn't a career for me, so I've enrolled in two business classes at the nearby community college. It turned out to be a good thing because Sam and his no-longer-an-almost-ex-wife finally decided to work through their issues and commit to their marriage. They put the pub up for sale, and moved closer to her family and her new job in Wilmington.

Seeing this as a good opportunity for me, I used the money my grandparents left me to put a down payment on the bar. Sam was excited to work with me on a fair price, knowing that what he'd done to build up his business would continue with me.

After talking a great deal and making preliminary plans with Liam and Cole, they decided to invest with me. So, not only have we become good friends, we're partners now too. I knew they were good guys, and going into business with them was a definitely a good decision. Together, we'll pull on our strengths to make the most of this new business venture. I have no doubt it will be successful. The coolest pub in town, with the best music, is only going to get better.

Today, Raina and I decide to make our way to the butterfly house at the science museum in Raleigh. The last time I was here, I ended up in the hospital and vowed never to come back, but since my brother is buried in a cemetery right outside of town, I couldn't really stay away forever. Visiting his grave for the first time since he passed was strange, but mildly comforting. Having Raina with me, talking to me, gave me a fresh perspective. I feel like I know he's okay now. It's important for Raina to visit her parents' grave occasionally, and it's easy to understand that now, after being at my brother's.

Walking hand in hand, we simply enjoy the sunshine and warm weather.

"This is such an amazing place. I haven't been here since I was a little girl," she says, bouncing on her toes and smiling.

"I've never been here, so you'll have to be my guide."

The beauty of this place doesn't compare to the look on Raina's face as she takes it all in. Her smile is infectious and her eyes glitter with happiness.

Raina

We walk into the large stone building and pay our entrance fee. Inside the air is warm and humid, and butterflies are flittering everywhere. It really is breathtaking. There are thousands of colorful flowers everywhere, luring the butterflies in to land on their petals. Huge green trees, and even a waterfall, fill the inside of this oasis. The ceiling is nothing but windows allowing the sunlight to filter through, like a beacon from Heaven. There is a small bench along the brick path, where we take a seat, taking in all the beauty around us. I hold out my hand and within minutes, two butterflies land gently on my warm skin. I can feel myself smiling, and my face lighting up with excitement.

"They're like the ones on the picture frame at the apartment." My eyes fill with tears, but this time I know they're tears of happiness. I stay completely still, mesmerized by the little creatures, not wanting them to fly away too soon.

I look to Zane and watch in surprise as he drops to the ground on one knee. With shaky hands, he pulls a small black jewelry box out of his pocket and looks at me, pretending he has nerves of steel. He breathes deeply and closes his eyes as he opens the box, revealing a beautiful, solitaire diamond. I remain completely still, most likely out of nervousness myself. I gently bring my hand down to my lap and yet, even with the movement, the butterflies remain.

"Raina, I have to be the luckiest man alive to still have you with me. We've been through so much together. And I am undeniably a stronger man because of you. I am happier than I've ever been because of you. I'm healing because of you. My heart is no longer my own and I can't think of anyone I would rather share it with. I want to make you happier than you've ever been and help you become even stronger than you already are. You are my once in a lifetime, baby. Will you be my forever? Will you marry me?"

Tears of happiness spill from my eyes. "Yes! Yes, I'll marry you."

His brilliant smile lights up an already illuminated room. My God, I love this man.

Zane takes my hand in his as the butterflies flutter away toward the rays of sun. Comfort and happiness make their way to his eyes as the stunning, yet simple, diamond ring slides onto my finger. The butterflies are back. This time, in my stomach.

"Rain, I can't tell you how happy I am. You've shown me more grace and more kindness that anyone I've ever known. I knew from the moment I started watching over you, that you were meant to be mine. I love you, baby."

There is no doubt in my mind that Zane has become an integral part of me. He makes my life whole again. He is the first thing I see at morning's light, and his arms are the last thing I feel at day's end. He gives my mind peace. He has become the very best part of me, and I have no doubt we are destined to be together. He pulls me close and wraps me in love and warmth, my security blanket. He is my forever. I am home.

~ The End ~

Acknowledgments

There is a myriad of people who have helped make this, my debut novel, possible. First and foremost, I would like to thank my husband. Your kindness, love, and support mean everything to me. You were there to lift me up when I was too scared to keep going, and there to encourage me when I was ready to throw in the towel. Twenty-five years of marriage and two kids later, you are still my rock, my go-to, and my forever.

I would like to thank my two amazing children (college students, actually) who endured dinners of boxed macaroni and cheese, as well as a variety of pizza (sometimes, no dinner at all) while this novel was being written, re-written, and finally published. Alex and Lawren, you are the light of my life and make my days shine. Your help (and the other Alex's too) with this project made it that much more special to me.

As for the rest of my family, I am so appreciative of all the support. You are my biggest cheerleaders and, throughout this past year, you have been very encouraging and support-ive. So, thank you for that!

To my gaggle of girlfriends on Facebook...my *One Bite at a Time* crew. Who would have ever guessed I'd have such amazing support from a group of ladies who didn't even know me when we first connected. I cannot thank you all enough for making me laugh, giving me advice and suggestions, and helping me hang in there when things seemed to be going all wrong. Your friendship means the world. And since we live all over the world, I guess that's a good thing.

Melissa and Jenn. Your input was invaluable, and you made my words better. Thank you, a million times over, for taking this baby and make it shine, for taking on a brand new author like me and supporting me the way you have. You believed in me when I questioned my own sanity. I think you both deserve a medal! At the very least, a bottle of wine.

I'd also like to thank Melissa, Kristin and MJ for Beta reading and providing such beneficial input that helped make Zane and Raina's story come to life.

And finally, I'd like to thank the bloggers, fellow authors, and most of all you, the readers, who took a chance on a new author and read my words.

Publishing this story was the scariest thing I've ever done. My anxiety hit an all time high, but with the love and support everyone has given me, I turned this dream of writing a book into a reality.

From the bottom of my heart, I thank each and every one of you.

About the Author

Olivia Stephen is an author of contemporary romance, a certified wine drinker and book lover. *Watch Over Her* is Olivia's debut novel. The mountains of Western Maryland is where Olivia calls home.

You can find more information on upcoming novels or follow Olivia Stephen on social media here:

www.facebook.com/oliviaspage

www.facebook.com/groups/oliviasallstars

www.instagram.com/oliviastephenauthor66

www.goodreads.com/author/show/18058409.Olivia_Stephen

Made in the
USA
Middletown, DE